GRACE PALEY was born and educated in New York, where she still lives. She has taught at Columbia University and at Sarah Lawrence; has published fiction in *New American Review*, *Esquire*, and *The Atlantic*, as well as in other periodicals; and is now at work on a novel.

"Her language is so wild and fanciful that from time to time it takes off into a realm that borders on the surreal; her vision is of sexy little girls, loving and bickering couples, envenomed suburbanites, yowling job-hunters in an America that is nutty but so recognizable that it hurts." —HARVEY SWADOS

"Her stories are shrewd, funny, and full of feeling: she has a girl's charm and a woman's strength; she is an exciting writer." —HERBERT GOLD

"Miss Paley is a natural all right. . . . She has a wonderful faculty of making everything in her stories seem new and unused." —The New York Times

The Little Disturbances of Man

GRACE PALEY

A PLUME BOOK

NEW AMERICAN LIBRARY

TIMES MIRROR

NEW YORK AND SCARBOROUGH, ONTARIO

PLUME TRADEMARK REG. U.S. PAT. OFF. AND FOREIGN COUNTRIES
REGISTERED TRADEMARK — MARCA REGISTRADA
HECHO EN CLINTON, MASS., U.S.A.

SIGNET, SIGNET CLASSICS, MENTOR,
PLUME and MERIDIAN BOOKS
are published *in the United States* by
The New American Library, Inc.,
1301 Avenue of the Americas, New York,
New York 10019
in Canada by
The New American Library of Canada Limited,
81 Mack Avenue, Scarborough, 704, Ontario

First Printing, May, 1973

5 6 7 8 9 10 11 12 13

PRINTED IN THE UNITED STATES OF AMERICA

Contents

Goodbye and Good Luck

I was popular in certain circles, says Aunt Rose. I wasn't no thinner then, only more stationary in the flesh. In time to come, Lillie, don't be surprised—change is a fact of God. From this no one is excused. Only a person like your mama stands on one foot, she don't notice how big her behind is getting and sings in the canary's ear for thirty years. Who's listening? Papa's in the shop. You and Seymour, thinking about yourself. So she waits in a spotless kitchen for a kind word and thinks—poor Rosie. . . .

Poor Rosie! If there was more life in my little sister, she would know my heart is a regular college of feelings and there is such information between my corset and me that her whole married life is a kindergarten.

Nowadays you could find me any time in a hotel, uptown or downtown. Who needs an apartment to live like a maid with a dustrag in the hand, sneezing? I'm in very good with the bus boys, it's more interesting than home, all kinds of people, everybody with a reason. . . .

And my reason, Lillie, is a long time ago I said to the forelady, "Missus, if I can't sit by the window, I can't sit." "If you can't sit, girlie," she says politely, "go stand on the street corner." And that's how I got unemployed in novelty wear.

For my next job I answered an ad which said: "Refined young lady, medium salary, cultural organization." I went by trolley to the address, the Russian Art Theater of Second Avenue where they played only the best Yiddish plays. They needed a ticket seller, someone like me, who likes the public but is very sharp on crooks. The man who interviewed me was the manager, a certain type.

Immediately he said: "Rosie Lieber, you surely got a build on you!"

"It takes all kinds, Mr. Krimberg."

"Don't misunderstand me, little girl," he said. "I appreciate, I appreciate. A young lady lacking fore and aft, her blood is so busy warming the toes and the finger tips, it don't have time to circulate where it's most required."

Everybody likes kindness. I said to him: "Only don't be fresh, Mr. Krimberg, and we'll make a good bargain."

We did: Nine dollars a week, a glass of tea every night, a free ticket once a week for Mama, and I could go watch rehearsals any time I want.

My first nine dollars was in the grocer's hands ready to move on already, when Krimberg said to me, "Rosie, here's a great gentleman, a member of this remarkable theater, wants to meet you, impressed no doubt by your big brown eyes."

And who was it, Lillie? Listen to me, before my very eyes was Volodya Vlashkin, called by the people of those days the Valentino of Second Avenue. I took one look, and I said to myself: Where did a Jewish boy grow up so big? "Just outside Kiev," he told me.

How? "My mama nursed me till I was six. I was the only boy in the village to have such health."

"My goodness, Vlashkin, six years old! She must have had shredded wheat there, not breasts, poor woman."

"My mother was beautiful," he said. "She had eyes like stars."

He had such a way of expressing himself, it brought tears.

To Krimberg, Vlashkin said after this introduction: "Who is responsible for hiding this wonderful young person in a cage?"

"That is where the ticket seller sells."

"So, David, go in there and sell tickets for a half hour. I have something in mind in regards to the future of this girl and this company. Go, David, be a good boy. And you, Miss Lieber, please, I suggest Feinberg's for a glass of tea. The rehearsals are long. I enjoy a quiet interlude with a friendly person."

So he took me there, Feinberg's, then around the corner, a place so full of Hungarians, it was deafening. In the back room was a table of honor for him. On the tablecloth embroidered by the lady of the house was "Here Vlashkin Eats." We finished one glass of tea in quietness, out of thirst, when I finally made up my mind what to say.

"Mr. Vlashkin, I saw you a couple weeks ago, even before I started working here, in *The Sea Gull*. Believe me, if I was that girl, I wouldn't look even for a minute on the young bourgeois fellow. He could fall out of the play altogether. How Chekhov could put him in the same play as you, I can't understand."

"You liked me?" he asked, taking my hand and kindly patting it. "Well, well, young people still like me . . . so, and you like the theater too? Good. And you, Rose, you

11

know you have such a nice hand, so warm to the touch, such a fine skin, tell me, why do you wear a scarf around your neck? You only hide your young, young throat. These are not olden times, my child, to live in shame."

"Who's ashamed?" I said, taking off the kerchief, but my hand right away went to the kerchief's place, because the truth is, it really was olden times, and I was still of a nature to melt with shame.

"Have some more tea, my dear."

"No, thank you, I am a samovar already."

"Dorfmann!" he hollered like a king. "Bring this child a seltzer with fresh ice!"

In weeks to follow I had the privilege to know him better and better as a person—also the opportunity to see him in his profession. The time was autumn; the theater full of coming and going. Rehearsing without end. After *The Sea Gull* flopped *The Salesman from Istanbul* played, a great success.

Here the ladies went crazy. On the opening night, in the middle of the first scene, one missus—a widow or her husband worked too long hours—began to clap and sing out, "Oi, oi, Vlashkin." Soon there was such a tumult, the actors had to stop acting. Vlashkin stepped forward. Only not Vlashkin to the eyes . . . a younger man with pitch-black hair, lively on restless feet, his mouth clever. A half a century later at the end of the play he came out again, a gray philosopher, a student of life from only reading books, his hands as smooth as silk. . . . I cried to think who I was—nothing—and such a man could look at me with interest.

Then I got a small raise, due to he kindly put in a good word for me, and also for fifty cents a night I was given the pleasure together with cousins, in-laws, and plain stage-struck kids to be part of a crowd scene and to see like he saw every single night the hundreds of pale faces waiting for his feelings to make them laugh or bend down their heads in sorrow.

The sad day came, I kissed my mama goodbye. Vlashkin helped me to get a reasonable room near the theater to be more free. Also my outstanding friend would have a place to recline away from the noise of the dressing rooms. She cried and she cried. "This is a different way of living, Mama," I said. "Besides, I am driven by love."

"You! You, a nothing, a rotten hole in a piece of cheese, are you telling me what is life?" she screamed.

Very insulted, I went away from her. But I am good-natured—you know fat people are like that—kind, and I thought to myself, poor Mama . . . it is true she got more of an idea of life than me. She married who she didn't like, a sick man, his spirit already swallowed up by God. He never washed. He had an unhappy smell. His teeth fell out, his hair disappeared, he got smaller, shriveled up little by little, till goodbye and good luck he was gone and only came to Mama's mind when she went to the mailbox under the stairs to get the electric bill. In memory of him and out of respect for mankind, I decided to live for love.

Don't laugh, you ignorant girl.

Do you think it was easy for me? I had to give Mama a little something. Ruthie was saving up together with your papa for linens, a couple knives and forks. In the morning I had to do piecework if I wanted to keep by myself. So I made flowers. Before lunch time every day a whole garden grew on my table.

13

This was my independence, Lillie dear, blooming, but it didn't have no roots and its face was paper.

Meanwhile Krimberg went after me too. No doubt observing the success of Vlashkin, he thought, "Aha, open sesame . . ." Others in the company similar. After me in those years were the following: Krimberg I mentioned. Carl Zimmer, played innocent young fellows with a wig. Charlie Peel, a Christian who fell in the soup by accident, a creator of beautiful sets. "Color is his middle name," says Vlashkin, always to the point.

I put this in to show you your fat old aunt was not crazy out of loneliness. In those noisy years I had friends among interesting people who admired me for reasons of youth and that I was a first-class listener.

The actresses—Raisele, Marya, Esther Leopold—were only interested in tomorrow. After them was the rich men, producers, the whole garment center; their past is a pincushion, future the eye of a needle.

Finally the day came, I no longer could keep my tact in my mouth. I said: "Vlashkin, I hear by carrier pigeon you have a wife, children, the whole combination."

"True, I don't tell stories. I make no pretense."

"That isn't the question. What is this lady like? It hurts me to ask, but tell me, Vlashkin . . . a man's life is something I don't clearly see."

"Little girl, I have told you a hundred times, this small room is the convent of my troubled spirit. Here I come to your innocent shelter to refresh myself in the midst of an agonized life."

"Ach, Vlashkin, serious, serious, who is this lady?"

"Rosie, she is a fine woman of the middle classes, a good mother to my children, three in number, girls all, a good cook, in her youth handsome, now no longer young. You see, could I be more frank? I entrust you, dear, with my soul."

It was some few months later at the New Year's ball of the Russian Artists Club, I met Mrs. Vlashkin, a woman with black hair in a low bun, straight and too proud. She sat at a small table speaking in a deep voice to whoever stopped a moment to converse. Her Yiddish was perfect, each word cut like a special jewel. I looked at her. She noticed me like she noticed everybody, cold like Christmas morning. Then she got tired. Vlashkin called a taxi and I never saw her again. Poor woman, she did not know I was on the same stage with her. The poison I was to her role, she did not know.

Later on that night in front of my door I said to Vlashkin, "No more. This isn't for me. I am sick from it all. I am no home breaker."

"Girlie," he said, "don't be foolish."

"No, no, goodbye, good luck," I said. "I am sincere."

So I went and stayed with Mama for a week's vacation and cleaned up all the closets and scrubbed the walls till the paint came off. She was very grateful, all the same her hard life made her say, "Now we see the end. If you live like a bum, you are finally a lunatic."

After this few days I came back to my life. When we met, me and Vlashkin, we said only hello and goodbye, and then for a few sad years, with the head we nodded as if to say, "Yes, yes, I know who you are."

Meanwhile in the field was a whole new strategy. Your mama and your grandmama brought around— boys. Your own father had a brother, you never even seen him. Ruben. A serious fellow, his idealism was his hat and his coat. "Rosie, I offer you a big new free happy unusual life." How? "With me, we will raise up the sands of Palestine to make a nation. That is the land of tomorrow for us Jews." "Ha-ha, Ruben, I'll go tomorrow then." "Rosie!" says Ruben. "We need strong women like you, mothers and farmers." "You don't fool me, Ruben, what you need is dray horses. But for that you need more money." "I don't like your attitude, Rose." "In that case, go and multiply. Goodbye."

Another fellow: Yonkel Gurstein, a regular sport, dressed to kill, with such an excitable nature. In those days—it looks to me like yesterday—the youngest girls wore undergarments like Battle Creek, Michigan. To him it was a matter of seconds. Where did he practice, a Jewish boy? Nowadays I suppose it is easier, Lillie? My goodness, I ain't asking you nothing—touchy, touchy. . . .

Well, by now you must know yourself, honey, whatever you do, life don't stop. It only sits a minute and dreams a dream.

While I was saying to all these silly youngsters "no, no, no," Vlashkin went to Europe and toured a few seasons . . . Moscow, Prague, London, even Berlin—already a pessimistic place. When he came back he wrote a book, you could get from the library even today, *The Jewish Actor Abroad.* If someday you're interested enough in my lonesome years, you could read it. You could absorb a flavor of the man from the book. No, no, I am not mentioned. After all, who am I?

When the book came out I stopped him in the street to say congratulations. But I am not a liar, so I pointed out, too, the egotism of many parts—even the critics said something along such lines.

"Talk is cheap," Vlashkin answered me. "But who are the critics? Tell me, do they create? Not to mention," he continues, "there is a line in Shakespeare in one of the plays from the great history of England. It says, 'Self-loving is not so vile a sin, my liege, as self-neglecting.' This idea also appears in modern times in the moralistic followers of Freud. . . . Rosie, are you listening? You asked a question. By the way, you look very well. How come no wedding ring?"

I walked away from this conversation in tears. But this talking in the street opened the happy road up for more discussions. In regard to many things. . . . For instance, the management—very narrow-minded—wouldn't give him any more certain young men's parts. Fools. What youngest man knew enough about life to be as young as him?

"Rosie, Rosie," he said to me one day, "I see by the clock on your rosy, rosy face you must be thirty."

"The hands are slow, Vlashkin. On a week before Thursday I was thirty-four."

"Is that so? Rosie, I worry about you. It has been on my mind to talk to you. You are losing your time. Do you understand it? A woman should not lose her time."

"Oi, Vlashkin, if you are my friend, what is time?"

For this he had no answer, only looked at me surprised. We went instead, full of interest but not with our former speed, up to my new place on Ninety-fourth Street. The same pictures on the wall, all of Vlashkin, only now everything painted red and black, which was stylish, and new upholstery.

A few years ago there was a book by another member of that fine company, an actress, the one that learned English very good and went uptown—Marya Kavkaz, in which she says certain things regarding Vlashkin. Such as, he was her lover for eleven years, she's not ashamed to write this down. Without respect for him, his wife and children, or even others who also may have feelings in the matter.

Now, Lillie, don't be surprised. This is called a fact of life. An actor's soul must be like a diamond. The more faces it got the more shining is his name. Honey, you will no doubt love and marry one man and have a couple kids and be happy forever till you die tired. More than that, a person like us don't have to know. But a great artist like Volodya Vlashkin . . . in order to make a job on the stage, he's got to practice. I understand it now, to him life is like a rehearsal.

Myself, when I saw him in *The Father-in-law*—an older man in love with a darling young girl, his son's wife, played by Raisele Maisel—I cried. What he said to this girl, how he whispered such sweetness, how all his hot feelings were on his face . . . Lillie, all this experience he had with me. The very words were the same. You can imagine how proud I was.

So the story creeps to an end.

I noticed it first on my mother's face, the rotten handwriting of time, scribbled up and down her cheeks, across her forehead back and forth—a child could read —it said, old, old, old. But it troubled my heart most to see these realities scratched on Vlashkin's wonderful expression.

First the company fell apart. The theater ended.

Esther Leopold died from being very aged. Krimberg had a heart attack. Marya went to Broadway. Also Raisele changed her name to Roslyn and was a big comical hit in the movies. Vlashkin himself, no place to go, retired. It said in the paper, "an actor without peer, he will write his memoirs and spend his last years in the bosom of his family among his thriving grandchildren, the apple of his wife's doting eye."

This is journalism.

We made for him a great dinner of honor. At this dinner I said to him, for the last time, I thought, "Goodbye, dear friend, topic of my life, now we part." And to myself I said further: Finished. This is your lonesome bed. A lady what they call fat and fifty. You made it personally. From this lonesome bed you will finally fall to a bed not so lonesome, only crowded with a million bones.

And now comes? Lillie, guess.

Last week, washing my underwear in the basin, I get a buzz on the phone. "Excuse me, is this the Rose Lieber formerly connected with the Russian Art Theater?"

"It is."

"Well, well, how do you do, Rose? This is Vlashkin."

"Vlashkin! Volodya Vlashkin?"

"In fact. How are you, Rose?"

"Living, Vlashkin, thank you."

"You are all right? Really, Rose? Your health is good? You are working?"

"My health, considering the weight it must carry, is first-class. I am back for some years now where I started, in novelty wear."

"Very interesting."

"Listen, Vlashkin, tell me the truth, what's on your mind?"

"My mind? Rosie, I am looking up an old friend, an old warmhearted companion of more joyful days. My circumstances, by the way, are changed. I am retired, as you know. Also I am a free man."

"What? What do you mean?"

"Mrs. Vlashkin is divorcing me."

"What come over her? Did you start drinking or something from melancholy?"

"She is divorcing me for adultery."

"But, Vlashkin, you should excuse me, don't be insulted, but you got maybe seventeen, eighteen years on me, and even me, all this nonsense—this daydreams and nightmares—is mostly for the pleasure of conversation alone."

"I pointed all this out to her. My dear, I said, my time is past, my blood is as dry as my bones. The truth is, Rose, she isn't accustomed to have a man around all day, reading out loud from the papers the interesting events of our time, waiting for breakfast, waiting for lunch. So all day she gets madder and madder. By nighttime a furious old lady gives me my supper. She has information from the last fifty years to pepper my soup. Surely there was a Judas in that theater, saying every day, 'Vlashkin, Vlashkin, Vlashkin . . .' and while my heart was circulating with his smiles he was on the wire passing the dope to my wife."

"Such a foolish end, Volodya, to such a lively story. What is your plans?"

"First, could I ask you for dinner and the theater—up-

town, of course? After this . . . we are old friends. I
have money to burn. What your heart desires. Others
are like grass, the north wind of time has cut out their
heart. Of you, Rosie, I recreate only kindness. What a
woman should be to a man, you were to me. Do you
think, Rosie, a couple of old pals like us could have
a few good times among the material things of this
world?"

My answer, Lillie, in a minute was altogether. "Yes,
yes, come up," I said. "Ask the room by the switchboard,
let us talk."

So he came that night and every night in the week,
we talked of his long life. Even at the end of time, a
fascinating man. And like men are, too, till time's end,
trying to get away in one piece.

"Listen, Rosie," he explains the other day. "I was married to my wife, do you realize, nearly half a century.
What good was it? Look at the bitterness. The more I
think of it, the more I think we would be fools to marry."

"Volodya Vlashkin," I told him straight, "when I was
young I warmed your cold back many a night, no questions asked. You admit it, I didn't make no demands. I
was softhearted. I didn't want to be called Rosie Lieber,
a breaker up of homes. But now, Vlashkin, you are a free
man. How could you ask me to go with you on trains to
stay in strange hotels, among Americans, not your wife?
Be ashamed."

So now, darling Lillie, tell this story to your mama
from your young mouth. She don't listen to a word from
me. She only screams, "I'll faint, I'll faint." Tell her after
all I'll have a husband, which, as everybody knows, a

woman should have at least one before the end of the story.

My goodness, I am already late. Give me a kiss. After all, I watched you grow from a plain seed. So give me a couple wishes on my wedding day. A long and happy life. Many years of love. Hug Mama, tell her from Aunt Rose, goodbye and good luck.

A Woman, Young and Old

My mother was born not too very long ago of my grandma, who named lots of others, girls and boys, all starting fresh. It wasn't love so much, my grandma said, but she never could call a spade a spade. She was imagination-minded, read stories all day and sighed all night, till my grandpa, to get near her at all, had to use that particular medium.

That was the basic trouble. My mother was sad to be so surrounded by brothers and sisters, none of them more good-natured than she. It's all part of the violence in the atmosphere is a theory—wars, deception, broken homes, all the irremediableness of modern life. To meet her problem my mother screams.

She swears she wouldn't scream if she had a man of her own, but all the aunts and uncles, solitary or wed, are noisy. My grandpa is not only noisy, he beats people up, that is to say—members of the family. He whacked my mother every day of her life. If anyone ever touched me, I'd reduce them to fall-out.

Grandma saves all her change for us. My uncle Johnson is in the nut house. The others are here and now, but Aunty Liz is seventeen and my mother talks to her as though she were totally grown up. Only the other day she told her she was just dying for a man, a real one, and was sick of raising two girls in a world just bristling with goddamn phallic symbols. Lizzy said yes, she knew how it was, time frittered by, and what you needed was a strong kind hand at the hem of your skirt. That's what the acoustics of this barn have to take.

My father, I have been told several hundred times, was a really stunning Latin. Full of *savoir-faire, joie de vivre,* and so forth. They were deeply and irrevocably in love till Joanna and I revoked everything for them. Mother doesn't want me to feel rejected, but she doesn't want to feel rejected herself, so she says *I* was too noisy and cried every single night. And then Joanna was the final blight and wanted titty all day *and* all night. ". . . a wife," he said, "is a beloved mistress until the children come and then . . ." He would just leave it hanging in French, but whenever I'd hear *les enfants,* I'd throw toys at him, guessing his intended slight. He said *les filles* instead, but I caught that petty evasion in no time. We pummeled him with noise and toys, but our affection was his serious burden is mother's idea, and one day he did not come home for supper.

Mother waited up reading *Le Monde,* but he did not come home at midnight to make love. He missed breakfast and lunch the next day. In fact, where is he now? Killed in the resistance, says Mother. A post card two weeks later told her and still tells us all, for that matter, whenever it's passed around: "I have been lonely for France for five years. Now for the rest of my life I must be lonely for you."

"You've been conned, Mother," I said one day while we were preparing dinner.

"Conned?" she muttered. "You speak a different language than me. You don't know a thing yet, you weren't even born. You know perfectly well, misfortune aside, I'd take another Frenchman—— Oh, Josephine," she continued, her voice reaching strictly for the edge of the sound barrier, "oh, Josephine, to these loathesomes in this miserable country I'm a joke, a real ha-ha. But over there they'd know me. They would just feel me boiling out to meet them. Lousy grammar and all, in French, I swear I could write Shakespeare."

I turned away in despair. I felt like crying.

"Don't laugh," she said, "someday I'll disappear Air France and surprise you all with a nice curly Frenchman just like your daddy. Oh, how you would have loved your father. A growing-up girl with a man like that in the vicinity constantly. You'd thank me."

"I thank you anyway, Mother dear," I replied, "but keep your taste in your own hatch. When I'm as old as Aunt Lizzy I might like American soldiers. Or a marine, I think. I already like some soldiers, especially Corporal Brownstar."

"Is *that* your idea of a man?" asked Mother, rowdy with contempt.

Then she reconsidered Corporal Brownstar. "Well, maybe you're right. Those powerful-looking boots . . . Very masculine."

"Oh?"

"I know, I know. I'm artistic and I sometimes hold two views at once. I realize that Lizzy's going around with him and it does something. Look at Lizzy and you see the girl your father saw. Just like me. Wonderful carriage. Marvelous muscle tone. She could have any man she wanted."

"She's already had some she wanted."

27

At that very moment my grandma, the nick-of-time banker, came in, proud to have saved $4.65 for us. "Whew, I'm so warm," she sighed. "Well, here it is. Now a nice dinner, Marvine, I beg of you, a little effort. Josie, run and get an avocado, and Marvine, please don't be small about the butter. And Josie dear, it's awful warm out and your mama won't mind. You're nearly a young lady. Would you like a sip of icy beer?"

Wasn't that respectful? To return the compliment I drank half a glass, though I hate that fizz. We broiled and steamed and sliced and chopped, and it was a wonderful dinner. I did the cooking and Mother did the sauces. We sicked her on with mouth-watering memories of another more gourmet time and, purely flattered, she made one sauce too many and we had it for dessert on saltines, with iced *café au lait*. While I cleared the dishes, Joanna, everybody's piece of fluff, sat on Grandma's lap telling her each single credible detail of her eight hours at summer day camp.

"Women," said Grandma in appreciation, "have been the pleasure and consolation of my entire life. From the beginning I cherished all the little girls with their clean faces and their listening ears. . . ."

"Men are different than women," said Joanna, and it's the only thing she says in this entire story.

"That's true," said Grandma, "it's the men that've always troubled me. Men and boys . . . I suppose I don't understand them. But think of it consecutively, all in a row, Johnson, Revere, and Drummond . . . after all, where did they start from but me? But all of them, all all all, each single one of them is gone, far away in heart and body."

"Ah, Grandma," I said, hoping to console, "they were all so grouchy, anyway. I don't miss them a bit."

Grandma gave me a miserable look. "Everyone's sons are like that," she explained. "First grouchy, then gone."

After that she sat in grieving sorrow. Joanna curled herself round the hassock at her feet, hugged it, and slept. Mother got her last week's copy of *Le Monde* out of the piano bench and calmed herself with a story about a farmer in Provence who had raped his niece and killed his mother and lived happily for thirty-eight years into respected old age before the nosy prefect caught up with him. She translated it into our derivative mother tongue while I did the dishes.

Nighttime came and communication was revived at last by our doorbell, which is full of initiative. It was Lizzy and she did bring Corporal Brownstar. We sent Joanna out for beer and soft drinks and the dancing started right away. He co-operatively danced with everyone. I slipped away to my room for a moment and painted a lot of lipstick neatly on my big mouth and hooked a walleyed brassière around my ribs to make him understand that I was older than Joanna.

He said to me, "You're peaches and cream, you're gonna be quite a girl someday, Alice in Wonderland."

"I am a girl already, Corporal."

"Uh *huh*," he said, squeezing my left bottom.

Lizzy passed the punch and handed out Ritz crackers and danced with Mother and Joanna whenever the corporal danced with me. She was delighted to see him so popular, and it just passed her happy head that he was the only man there. At the peak of the evening he said: "You may all call me Browny."

We sang air-force songs then until 2 A.M., and Grandma said the songs hadn't changed much since her war. "The soldiers are younger though," she said. "Son, you look like your mother is still worried about you."

"No reason to worry about me, I got a lot of irons in the fire. I get advanced all the time, as a matter of fact. Stem to stern," he said, winking at Lizzy, "I'm O.K. . . . By the way," he continued, "could you folks put me up? I wouldn't mind sleeping on the floor."

"The floor?" expostulated Mother. "Are you out of your mind? A soldier of the Republic. My God! We have a cot. You know . . . an army cot. Set it up and sleep the sleep of the just, Corporal."

"Oh, goodness," Grandma yawned, "talking about bed—Marvine, your dad must be home by now. I'd better be getting back."

Browny decided in a courteous way to take Lizzy and Grandma home. By the time he returned, Mother and Joanna had wrapped their lonesome arms around each other and gone to sleep.

I sneakily watched him from behind the drapes scrubbing himself down without consideration for his skin. Then, shining and naked, he crawled between the sheets in totality.

I unshod myself and tiptoed into the kitchen. I poured him a cold beer. I came straight to him and sat down by his side. "Here's a nice beer, Browny. I thought you might be hot after such a long walk."

"Why, thanks, Alice Palace Pudding and Pie, I happen to be pretty damn hot. You're a real pal."

He heaved himself up and got that beer into his gut in one gulp. I looked at him down to his belly button. He put the empty glass on the floor and grinned at me. He burped into my face for a joke and then I had to speak the truth. "Oh, Browny," I said, "I just love you so." I threw my arms around his middle and leaned my face into the golden hairs of his chest.

"Hey, pudding, take it easy. I like you too. You're a doll."

Then I kissed him right on the mouth.

"Josephine, who the hell taught you that?"

"I taught myself. I practiced on my wrist. See?"

"Josephine!" he said again. "Josephine, you're a liar. You're one hell of a liar!"

After that his affection increased, and he hugged me too and kissed me right on the mouth.

"Well," I kidded, "who taught you that? Lizzy?"

"Shut up," he said, and the more he loved me the less he allowed of conversation.

I lay down beside him, and I was really surprised the way a man is transformed by his feelings. He loved me all over myself, and to show I understood his meaning I whispered: "Browny, what do you want? Browny, do you want to do it?"

Well! He jumped out of bed then and flapped the sheet around his shoulders and groaned, "Oh, Christ. . . . Oh," he said, "I could be arrested. I could be picked up by M.P.'s and spend the rest of my life in jail." He looked at me. "For God's sakes button your shirt. Your mother'll wake up in a minute."

"Browny, what's the matter?"

"You're a child and you're too damn smart for your own good. Don't you understand? This could ruin my whole life."

"But, Browny . . ."

"The trouble I could get into! I could be busted.
You're a baby. It's a joke. A person could marry a baby
like you, but it's criminal to lay a hand on your shoulder.
That's funny, ha-ha-ha."

"Oh, Browny, I would love to be married to you."

He sat down at the edge of the cot and drew me to
his lap. "Gee, what a funny kid you are. You really like
me so much?"

"I love you. I'd be a first-class wife, Browny—do you
realize I take care of this whole house? When Mother
isn't working, she spends her whole time mulling over
Daddy. I'm the one who does Joanna's hair every day.
I iron her dresses. I could even have a baby for you,
Browny, I know just how to——"

"No! Oh no. Don't let anyone ever talk you into that.
Not till you're eighteen. You ought to stay tidy as a doll
and not strain your skin at least till you're eighteen."

"Browny, don't you get lonesome in that camp? I
mean if Lizzy isn't around and I'm not around . . .
Don't you think I have a nice figure?"

"Oh, I guess . . ." he laughed, and put his hand
warmly under my shirt. "It's pretty damn nice, considering it ain't even quite done."

I couldn't hold my desire down, and I kissed him
again right into his talking mouth and smack against his
teeth. "Oh, Browny, I would take care of you."

"O.K., O.K.," he said, pushing me kindly away. "O.K.,
now listen, go to sleep before we really cook up a stew.
Go to sleep. You're a sweet kid. Sleep it off. You ain't
even begun to see how wide the world is. It's a surprise
even to a man like me."

"But my mind is settled."

"Go to sleep, go sleep," he said, still holding my hand and patting it. "You look almost like Lizzy now."

"Oh, but I'm different. I know exactly what I want."

"Go to sleep, little girl," he said for the last time. I took his hand and kissed each brown finger tip and then ran into my room and took all my clothes off and, as bare as my lonesome soul, I slept.

The next day was Saturday and I was glad. Mother is a waitress all weekend at the Paris Coffee House, where she has been learning French from the waiters ever since Daddy disappeared. She's lucky because she really loves her work; she's crazy about the customers, the coffee, the décor, and is only miserable when she gets home.

I gave her breakfast on the front porch at about 10 A.M. and Joanna walked her to the bus. "Cook the corporal some of those frozen sausages," she called out in her middle range.

I hoped he'd wake up so we could start some more love, but instead Lizzy stepped over our sagging threshold. "Came over to fix Browny some breakfast," she said efficiently.

"Oh?" I looked her childlike in the eye. "I think *I* ought to do it, Aunty Liz, because he and I are probably getting married. Don't you think I ought to in that case?"

"What? Say that slowly, Josephine."

"You heard me, Aunty Liz."

She flopped in a dirndl heap on the stairs. "*I* don't

even feel old enough to get married and *I've* been seventeen since Christmas time. Did he really ask you?"

"We've been talking about it," I said, and that was true. "I'm in love with him, Lizzy." Tears prevented my vision.

"Oh, love . . . I've been in love twelve times since I was your age."

"Not me, I've settled on Browny. I'm going to get a job and send him to college after his draft is over. . . . He's very smart."

"Oh, smart . . . everybody's smart."

"No, they are not."

When she left I kissed Browny on both eyes, like the Sleeping Beauty, and he stretched and woke up in a conflagration of hunger.

"Breakfast, breakfast, breakfast," he bellowed.

I fed him and he said, "Wow, the guys would really laugh, me thiefin' the cradle this way."

"Don't feel like that. I make a good impression on people, Browny. There've been lots of men more grown than you who've made a fuss over me."

"Ha-ha," he remarked.

I made him quit that kind of laughing and started him on some kisses, and we had a cheerful morning.

"Browny," I said at lunch, "I'm going to tell Mother we're getting married."

"Don't she have enough troubles of her own?"

"No, no," I said. "She's all for love. She's crazy about it."

"Well, think about it a minute, baby face. After all, I might get shipped out to some troubled area and be knocked over by a crazy native. You read about something like that every day. Anyway, wouldn't it be fun to have a real secret engagement for a while? How about it?"

"Not me," I said, remembering everything I'd ever heard from Liz about the opportunism of men, how they will sometimes dedicate with seeming good will thirty days and nights, sleeping and waking, of truth and deceit to the achievement of a moment's pleasure. "Secret engagement! Some might agree to a plan like that, but not me."

Then I knew he liked me, because he walked around the table and played with the curls of my home permanent a minute and whispered, "The guys would really laugh, but I get a big bang out of you."

Then I wasn't sure he liked me, because he looked at his watch and asked it: "Where the hell is Lizzy?"

I had to do the shopping and put off some local merchants in a muddle of innocence, which is my main Saturday chore. I ran all the way. It didn't take very long, but as I rattled up the stairs and into the hall, I heard the thumping tail of a conversation. Browny was saying, "It's your fault, Liz."

"I couldn't care less," she said. "I suppose you get something out of playing around with a child."

"Oh no, you don't get it at all . . ."

"I can't say I want it."

"Goddamnit," said Browny, "you don't listen to a person. I think you stink."

"Really?" Turning to go, she smashed the screen door in my face and jammed my instep with the heel of her lavender pump.

"Tell your mother we will," Browny yelled when he

saw me. "She stinks, that Liz, goddamnit. Tell your mother tonight."

I did my best during that passing afternoon to make Browny more friendly. I sat on his lap and he drank beer and tickled me. I laughed, and pretty soon I understood the game and how it had to have variety and ran shrieking from him till he could catch me in a comfortable place, the living-room sofa or my own bedroom.

"You're O.K.," he said. "You are. I'm crazy about you, Josephine. You're a lot of fun."

So that night at nine-fifteen when mother came home I made her some iced tea and cornered her in the kitchen and locked the door. "I want to tell you something about me and Corporal Brownstar. Don't say a word, Mother. We're going to be married."

"What?" she said. "Married?" she screeched. "Are you crazy? You can't even get a job without working papers yet. You can't even get working papers. You're a baby. Are you kidding me? You're my little fish. You're not fourteen yet."

"Well, I decided we could wait until next month when I will be fourteen. Then, I decided, we can get married."

"You can't, my God! Nobody gets married at fourteen, nobody, nobody. I don't know a soul."

"Oh, Mother, people do, you always see them in the paper. The worst that could happen is it would get in the paper."

"But I didn't realize you had much to do with him. Isn't he Lizzy's? That's not nice—to take him away from her. That's a rotten sneaky trick. You're a sneak. Women should stick together. Didn't you learn anything yet?"

"Well, she doesn't want to get married and I do. And

it's essential to Browny to get married. He's a very clean-living boy, and when his furlough's over he doesn't want to go back to those camp followers and other people's wives. You have to appreciate that in him, Mother —it's a quality."

"You're a baby," she droned. "You're my slippery little fish."

Browny rattled the kitchen doorknob ten minutes too early.

"Oh, come in," I said, disgusted.

"How's stuff? Everything settled? What do you say, Marvine?"

"I say shove it, Corporal! What's wrong with Lizzy? You and she were really beautiful together. You looked like twin stars in the summer sky. Now I realize I don't like your looks much. Who's your mother and father? I never even heard much about them. For all I know, you got an uncle in Alcatraz. And your teeth are in terrible shape. I thought the Army takes care of things like that. You just don't look so hot to me."

"No reason to be personal, Marvine."

"But she's a baby. What if she becomes pregnant and bubbles up her entire constitution? This isn't India. Did you ever read what happened to the insides of those Indian child brides?"

"Oh, he's very gentle, Mother."

"What?" she said, construing the worst.

That conference persisted for about two hours. We drank a couple of pitcherfuls of raspberry Kool-Aid we'd been saving for Joanna's twelfth birthday party the next day. No one had a dime, and we couldn't find Grandma.

Later on, decently before midnight, Lizzy showed

up. She had a lieutenant (j.g.) with her and she introduced him around as Sid. She didn't introduce him to Browny, because she has stated time and time again that officers and enlisted men ought not to mix socially. As soon as the lieutenant took Mother's hand in greeting, I could see he was astonished. He began to perspire visibly in long welts down his back and in the gabardine armpits of his summer uniform. Mother was in one of those sullen, indolent moods which really put a fire under some men. She was just beady to think of my stubborn decision and how my life contained the roots of excitement.

"France is where I belong," she murmured to him. "Paris, Marseille, places like that, where men like women and don't chase little girls."

"I have a lot of sympathy with the Gallic temperament and I do like a real woman," he said hopefully.

"Sympathy is not enough." Her voice rose to the requirements of her natural disposition. "Empathy is what I need. The empathy of a true friend is what I have lived without for years."

"Oh yes, I feel all that, empathy too," he fell deeply into his heart, from which he could scarcely be heard. . . . "I like a woman who's had some contact with life, cradled little ones, felt the pangs of birth, known the death of loved ones. . . ."

". . . and of love," she added sadly. "That's unusual in a young good-looking man."

"Yet that's my particular preference."

Lizzy, Browny, and I borrowed a dollar from him while he sat in idyllic stupor and we wandered out for some ice cream. We took Joanna because we were sorry to have drunk up her whole party. When we returned with a bottle of black-raspberry soda, no one was in sight. "I'm beginning to feel like a procurer," said Lizzy.

That's how come Mother finally said yes. Her moral turpitude took such a lively turn that she gave us money for a Wassermann. She called Dr. Gilmar and told him to be gentle with the needles. "It's my own little girl, Doctor. Little Josie that you pulled right out of me yourself. She's so headstrong. Oh, Doctor, remember me and Charles? She's a rough little customer, just like me."

Due to the results of this test, which is a law, and despite Browny's disbelief, we could not get married. Grandma, always philosophical with the advantage of years, said that young men sowing wild oats were often nipped in the bud, so to speak, and that modern science would soon unite us. Ha-ha-ha, I laugh in recollection.

Mother never even noticed. It passed her by completely, because of large events in her own life. When Browny left for camp drowned in penicillin and damp with chagrin, she gave him a giant jar of Loft's Sour Balls and a can of walnut rum tobacco.

Then she went ahead with her own life. Without any of the disenchantment Browny and I had suffered, the lieutenant and Mother got married. We were content, all of us, though it's common knowledge that she has never been divorced from Daddy. The name next to hers on the marriage license is Sidney LaValle, Jr., Lieut. (j.g.), U.S.N. An earlier, curlier generation of LaValles came to Michigan from Quebec, and Sid has a couple of usable idioms in Mother's favorite tongue.

I have received one card from Browny. It shows an

aerial view of Joplin, Mo. It says: "Hi, kid, chin up, love, Browny. P.S. Health improved."

Living as I do on a turnpike of discouragement, I am glad to hear the incessant happy noises in the next room. I enjoyed hugging with Browny's body, though I don't believe I was more to him than a hope for civilian success. Joanna has moved in with me. Though she grinds her teeth well into daylight, I am grateful for her company. Since I have been engaged, she looks up to me. She is a real cuddly girl.

The Pale Pink Roast

Pale green greeted him, grubby buds for nut trees. Packed with lunch, Peter strode into the park. He kicked aside the disappointed acorns and endowed a grand admiring grin to two young girls.

Anna saw him straddling the daffodils, a rosy man in about the third flush of youth. He got into Judy's eye too. Acquisitive and quick, she screamed, "There's Daddy!"

Well, that's who he was, mouth open, addled by visions. He was unsettled by a collusion of charm, a conspiracy of curly hairdos and shiny faces. A year ago, in plain view, Anna had begun to decline into withering years, just as he swelled to the maximum of manhood, spitting pipe smoke, patched with tweed, an advertisement of a lover who startled men and detained the ladies.

Now Judy leaped over the back of a bench and lunged into his arms. "Oh, Peter dear," she whispered, "I didn't even know you were going to meet us."

"God, you're getting big, kiddo. Where's your teeth?" he asked. He hugged her tightly, a fifty-pound sack of his very own. "Say, Judy, I'm glad you still have a pussycat's sniffy nose and a pussycat's soft white fur."

"I do not," she giggled.

"Oh yes," he said. He dropped her to her springy hind

legs but held onto one smooth front paw. "But you'd better keep your claws in or I'll drop you right into the Hudson River."

"Aw, Peter," said Judy, "quit it."

Peter changed the subject and turned to Anna. "You don't look half bad, you know."

"Thank you," she replied politely, "neither do you."

"Look at me, I'm a real outdoorski these days."

She allowed thirty seconds of silence, into which he turned, singing like a summer bird, "We danced around the Maypole, the Maypole, the Maypole . . .

"Well, when'd you get in?" he asked.

"About a week ago."

"You never called."

"Yes, I did, Peter. I called you at least twenty-seven times. You're never home. Petey must be in love somewhere, I said to myself."

"What is this thing," he sang in tune, "called love?"

"Peter, I want you to do me a favor," she started again. "Peter, could you take Judy for the weekend? We've just moved to this new place and I have a lot of work to do. I just don't want her in my hair. Peter?"

"Ah, that's why you called."

"Oh, for godsakes," Anna said. "I really called to ask you to become my lover. That's the real reason."

"O.K., O.K. Don't be bitter, Anna." He stretched forth a benedicting arm. "Come in peace, go in peace. Of course I'll take her. I like her. She's my kid."

"Bitter?" she asked.

Peter sighed. He turned the palms of his hands up as though to guess at rain. Anna knew him, theme and choreography. The sunshiny spring afternoon seeped

44

through his fingers. He looked up at the witnessing heavens to keep what he could. He dropped his arms and let the rest go.

"O.K.," he said. "Let's go. I'd like to see your place. I'm full of ideas. You should see my living room, Anna. I might even go into interior decorating if things don't pick up. Come on. I'll get the ladder out of the basement. I could move a couple of trunks. I'm crazy about heavy work. You get out of life what you put into it. Right? Let's ditch the kid. I'm not your enemy."

"Who is?" she asked.

"Off my back, Anna. I mean it. I'll get someone to keep an eye on Judy. Just shut up." He searched for a familiar face among the Sunday strollers. "Hey, you," he finally called to an old pal on whom two chicks were leaning. "Hey, you glass-eyed louse, c'mere."

"Not just any of your idiot friends," whispered Anna, enraged.

All three soft-shoed it over to Peter. They passed out happy hellos, also a bag of dried apricots. Peter spoke to one of the girls. He patted her little-boy haircut. "Well, well, baby, you have certainly changed. You must have had a very good winter."

"Oh yes, thanks," she admitted.

"Say, be my friend, doll, will you? There's Judy over there. Remember? She was nuts about you when she was little. How about it? Keep an eye on her about an hour or two?"

"Sure, Petey, I'd love to. I'm not busy today. Judy! She was cute. I was nuts about her."

"Anna," said Peter, "this is Louie; she was a real friend

45

that year you worked. She helped me out with Judy. She was great, a lifesaver."

"You're Anna," Louie said hospitably. "Oh, I think Judy's cute. We were nuts about each other. You have one smart kid. She's *really* smart."

"Thank you," said Anna.

Judy had gone off to talk to the ice cream man. She returned licking a double-lime Popsicle. "You have to give him ten cents," she said. "He didn't even remember me to give me trust."

Suddenly she saw Louie. "Oooh!" she shrieked. "It's Louie. Louie, Louie, Louie!" They pinched each other's cheeks, rubbed noses like the Eskimoses, and fluttered lashes like kissing angels do. Louie looked around proudly. "Gee whiz, the kid didn't forget me. How do you like that?"

Peter fished in his pockets for some change. Louie said, "Don't be ridiculous. It's on me." "O.K., girls," Peter said. "You two go on. Live it up. Eat supper out. Enjoy yourselves. Keep in touch."

"I guess they do know each other," said Anna, absolutely dispirited, waving goodbye.

"There!" said Peter. "If you want to do things, do things."

He took her arm. His other elbow cut their way through a gathering clutter of men and boys. "Going, going, gone," he said. "So long, fellows."

Within five minutes Anna unlocked the door of her new apartment, her snappy city leasehold, with a brand-new key.

In the wide foyer, on the parquet path narrowed by

rows of cardboard boxes, Peter stood stock-still and whistled a dozen bars of Beethoven's Fifth Symphony. "Mama," he moaned in joy, "let me live!"

A vista of rooms and doors to rooms, double glass doors, single hard-oak doors, narrow closet doors, a homeful of rooms wired with hallways stretched before. "Oh, Anna, it's a far cry . . . Who's paying for it?"

"Not you; don't worry."

"That's not the point, Mary and Joseph!" He waved his arms at a chandelier. "Now, Anna, I like to see my friends set up this way. You think I'm kidding."

"*I'm* kidding," said Anna.

"Come on, what's really cooking? You look so great, you look like a chick on the sincere make. Playing it cool and living it warm, you know . . ."

"Quit dreaming, Petey," she said irritably. But he had stripped his back to his undershirt and had started to move records into record cabinets. He stopped to say, "How about me putting up the Venetian blinds?" Then she softened and offered one kindness: "Peter, you're the one who really looks wonderful. You look just—well—healthy."

"I take care of myself, Anna. That's why. Vegetables, high proteins. I'm not the night owl I was. Grapefruits, sunlight, oh sunlight, that's my dear love now."

"You always did take care of yourself, Peter."

"No, Anna, this is different." He stopped and settled on a box of curtains. "I mean it's not egocentric and selfish, the way I used to be. Now it has a real philosophical basis. Don't mix me up with biology. Look at me, what do you see?"

Anna had read that cannibals, tasting man, saw him thereafter as the great pig, the pale pink roast.

"Peter, Peter, pumpkin eater," Anna said.

"Ah no, that's not what I mean. You know what you see? A structure of flesh. You know when it hit me? About two years ago, around the time we were breaking up, you and me. I took my grandpa to the bathroom one time when I was over there visiting—you remember him, Anna, that old jerk, the one that was so mad, he didn't want to die. . . . I was leaning on the door; he was sitting on the pot concentrating on his guts. Just to make conversation—I thought it'd help him relax—I said, 'Pop? Pop, if you had it all to do over again, what would you do different? Any real hot tips?'

"He came up with an answer right away. 'Peter,' he said, 'I'd go to a gym every goddamn day of my life; the hell with the job, the hell with the women. Peter, I'd build my body up till God hisself wouldn't know how to tear it apart. Look at me Peter,' he said. 'I been a mean sonofabitch the last fifteen years. Why? I'll tell you why. This structure, this . . . this thing'—he pinched himself across his stomach and his knees—'this me'—he cracked himself sidewise across his jaw—'this is got to be maintained. The reason is, Peter: *It is the dwelling place of the soul.* In the end, long life is the reward, strength, and beauty.'"

"Oh, Peter!" said Anna. "Are you working?"

"Man," said Peter, "you got the same itsy-bitsy motivations. Of course I'm working. How the hell do you think I live? Did you get your eight-fifty a week out in Scroungeville or not?"

"Eight-fifty is right."

"O.K., O.K. Then listen. I have a vitamin compound that costs me twelve-eighty a hundred. Fifty dollars a year for basic maintenance and repair."

"Did the old guy die?"

"Mother! Yes! Of course he died."

"I'm sorry. He wasn't so bad. He liked Judy."

"Bad or good, Anna, he got his time in, he lived long enough to teach the next generation. By the way, I don't think you've put on an ounce."

"Thanks."

"And the kid looks great. You do take good care of her. You were always a good mother. I'll bet you broil her stuff and all."

"Sometimes," she said.

"Let her live in the air," said Peter. "I bet you do. Let her love her body."

"Let her," said Anna sadly.

"To work, to work, where strike committees shirk," sang Peter. "*Is* the ladder in the cellar?"

"No, no, in that kitchen closet. The real tall closet."

Then Peter put up the Venetian blinds, followed by curtains. He distributed books among the available bookcases. He glued the second drawer of Judy's bureau. Although all the furniture had not been installed, there were shelves for Judy's toys. He had no trouble with them at all. He whistled while he worked.

Then he swept the debris into a corner of the kitchen. He put a pot of coffee on the stove. "Coffee?" he called. "In a minute," Anna said. He stabilized the swinging kitchen door and came upon Anna, winding a clock in the living room whose wide windows on the world he had personally draped. "Busy, busy," he said.

49

Like a good and happy man increasing his virtue, he kissed her. She did not move away from him. She remained in the embrace of his right arm, her face nuzzling his shoulder, her eyes closed. He tipped her chin to look and measure opportunity. She could not open her eyes. Honorably he searched, but on her face he met no quarrel.

She was faint and leaden, a sure sign in Anna, if he remembered correctly, of passion. "Shall we dance?" he asked softly, a family joke. With great care, a patient lover, he undid the sixteen tiny buttons of her pretty dress and in Judy's room on Judy's bed he took her at once without a word. Afterward, having established tenancy, he rewarded her with kisses. But he dressed quickly because he was obligated by the stories of his life to remind her of transience.

"Petey," Anna said, having drawn sheets and blankets to her chin. "Go on into the kitchen. I think the coffee's all boiled out."

He started a new pot. Then he returned to help her with the innumerable little cloth buttons. "Say, Anna, this dress is wild. It must've cost a dime."

"A quarter," she said.

"You know, we could have some pretty good times together every now and then if you weren't so damn resentful."

"Did you have a real good time, Petey?"

"Oh, the best," he said, kissing her lightly. "You know, I like the way your hair is now," he said.

"I have it done once a week."

"Hey, say it pays, baby. It does wonders. What's up, what's up? That's what I want to know. Where'd the classy TV come from? And that fabulous desk . . . Say, somebody's an operator."

"My husband is," said Anna.

Petey sat absolutely still, but frowned, marking his clear forehead with vertical lines of pain. Consuming the black fact, gritting his teeth to retain it, he said, "My God, Anna! That was a terrible thing to do."

"I thought it was so great."

"Oh, Anna, that's not the point. You should have said something first. Where is he? Where is this stupid son-ofabitch while his wife is getting laid?"

"He's in Rochester. That's where I met him. He's a lovely person. He's moving his business. It takes time. Peter, please. He'll be here in a couple of days."

"You're great, Anna. Man, you're great. You wiggle your ass. You make a donkey out of me and him both. You could've said no. No—excuse me, Petey—no. I'm not that hard up. Why'd you do it? Revenge? Meanness? Why?"

He buttoned his jacket and moved among the cardboard boxes and the new chairs, looking for a newspaper or a package. He hadn't brought a thing. He stopped before the hallway mirror to brush his hair. "That's it!" he said, and walked slowly to the door.

"Where are you going, Peter?" Anna called across the foyer, a place for noisy children and forgotten umbrellas. "Wait a minute, Peter. Honest to God, listen to me, I did it for love."

He stopped to look at her. He looked at her coldly.

Anna was crying. "I really mean it, Peter, I did it for love."

"Love?" he asked. "Really?" He smiled. He was embarrassed but happy. "Well!" he said. With the fingers of both hands he tossed her a kiss.

"Oh, Anna, then good night," he said. "You're a good kid. Honest, I wish you the best, the best of everything, the very best."

In no time at all his cheerful face appeared at the door of the spring dusk. In the street among peaceable strangers he did a handstand. Then easy and impervious, in full control, he cartwheeled eastward into the source of night.

The Loudest Voice

There is a certain place where dumb-waiters boom, doors slam, dishes crash; every window is a mother's mouth bidding the street shut up, go skate somewhere else, come home. My voice is the loudest.

There, my own mother is still as full of breathing as me and the grocer stands up to speak to her. "Mrs. Abramowitz," he says, "people should not be afraid of their children."

"Ah, Mr. Bialik," my mother replies, "if you say to her or her father 'Ssh,' they say, 'In the grave it will be quiet.'"

"From Coney Island to the cemetery," says my papa. "It's the same subway; it's the same fare."

I am right next to the pickle barrel. My pinky is making tiny whirlpools in the brine. I stop a moment to announce: "Campbell's Tomato Soup. Campbell's Vegetable Beef Soup. Campbell's S-c-otch Broth . . ."

"Be quiet," the grocer says, "the labels are coming off."

"Please, Shirley, be a little quiet," my mother begs me.

In that place the whole street groans: Be quiet! Be quiet! but steals from the happy chorus of my inside self not a tittle or a jot.

There, too, but just around the corner, is a red brick building that has been old for many years. Every morn-

55

ing the children stand before it in double lines which must be straight. They are not insulted. They are waiting anyway.

I am usually among them. I am, in fact, the first, since I begin with "A."

One cold morning the monitor tapped me on the shoulder. "Go to Room 409, Shirley Abramowitz," he said. I did as I was told. I went in a hurry up a down staircase to Room 409, which contained sixth-graders. I had to wait at the desk without wiggling until Mr. Hilton, their teacher, had time to speak.

After five minutes he said, "Shirley?"

"What?" I whispered.

He said, "My! My! Shirley Abramowitz! They told me you had a particularly loud, clear voice and read with lots of expression. Could that be true?"

"Oh yes," I whispered.

"In that case, don't be silly; I might very well be your teacher someday. Speak up, speak up."

"Yes," I shouted.

"More like it," he said. "Now, Shirley, can you put a ribbon in your hair or a bobby pin? It's too messy."

"Yes!" I bawled.

"Now, now, calm down." He turned to the class. "Children, not a sound. Open at page 39. Read till 52. When you finish, start again." He looked me over once more. "Now, Shirley, you know, I suppose, that Christmas is coming. We are preparing a beautiful play. Most of the parts have been given out. But I still need a child with a strong voice, lots of stamina. Do you know what stamina is? You do? Smart kid. You know, I heard you read 'The Lord is my shepherd' in Assembly yesterday.

I was very impressed. Wonderful delivery. Mrs. Jordan, your teacher, speaks highly of you. Now listen to me, Shirley Abramowitz, if you want to take the part and be in the play, repeat after me, 'I swear to work harder than I ever did before.'"

I looked to heaven and said at once, "Oh, I swear." I kissed my pinky and looked at God.

"That is an actor's life, my dear," he explained. "Like a soldier's, never tardy or disobedient to his general, the director. Everything," he said, "absolutely everything will depend on you."

That afternoon, all over the building, children scraped and scrubbed the turkeys and the sheaves of corn off the schoolroom windows. Goodbye Thanksgiving. The next morning a monitor brought red paper and green paper from the office. We made new shapes and hung them on the walls and glued them to the doors.

The teachers became happier and happier. Their heads were ringing like the bells of childhood. My best friend Evie was prone to evil, but she did not get a single demerit for whispering. We learned "Holy Night" without an error. "How wonderful!" said Miss Glacé, the student teacher. "To think that some of you don't even speak the language!" We learned "Deck the Halls" and "Hark! The Herald Angels". . . . They weren't ashamed and we weren't embarrassed.

Oh, but when my mother heard about it all, she said to my father: "Misha, you don't know what's going on there. Cramer is the head of the Tickets Committee."

"Who?" asked my father. "Cramer? Oh yes, an active woman."

"Active? Active has to have a reason. Listen," she said

sadly, "I'm surprised to see my neighbors making tra-la-la for Christmas."

My father couldn't think of what to say to that. Then he decided: "You're in America! Clara, you wanted to come here. In Palestine the Arabs would be eating you alive. Europe you had pogroms. Argentina is full of Indians. Here you got Christmas. . . . Some joke, ha?"

"Very funny, Misha. What is becoming of you? If we came to a new country a long time ago to run away from tyrants, and instead we fall into a creeping pogrom, that our children learn a lot of lies, so what's the joke? Ach, Misha, your idealism is going away."

"So is your sense of humor."

"That I never had, but idealism you had a lot of."

"I'm the same Misha Abramovitch, I didn't change an iota. Ask anyone."

"Only ask me," says my mama, may she rest in peace. "I got the answer."

Meanwhile the neighbors had to think of what to say too.

Marty's father said: "You know, he has a very important part, my boy."

"Mine also," said Mr. Sauerfeld.

"Not my boy!" said Mrs. Klieg. "I said to him no. The answer is no. When I say no! I mean no!"

The rabbi's wife said, "It's disgusting!" But no one listened to her. Under the narrow sky of God's great wisdom she wore a strawberry-blond wig.

Every day was noisy and full of experience. I was Right-hand Man. Mr. Hilton said: "How could I get along without you, Shirley?"

He said: "Your mother and father ought to get down

on their knees every night and thank God for giving them a child like you."

He also said: "You're absolutely a pleasure to work with, my dear, dear child."

Sometimes he said: "For God's sakes, what did I do with the script? Shirley! Shirley! Find it."

Then I answered quietly: "Here it is, Mr. Hilton."

Once in a while, when he was very tired, he would cry out: "Shirley, I'm just tired of screaming at those kids. Will you tell Ira Pushkov not to come in till Lester points to that star the second time?"

Then I roared: "Ira Pushkov, what's the matter with you? Dope! Mr. Hilton told you five times already, don't come in till Lester points to that star the second time."

"Ach, Clara," my father asked, "what does she do there till six o'clock she can't even put the plates on the table?"

"Christmas," said my mother coldly.

"Ho! Ho!" my father said. "Christmas. What's the harm? After all, history teaches everyone. We learn from reading this is a holiday from pagan times also, candles, lights, even Chanukah. So we learn it's not altogether Christian. So if they think it's a private holiday, they're only ignorant, not patriotic. What belongs to history, belongs to all men. You want to go back to the Middle Ages? Is it better to shave your head with a secondhand razor? Does it hurt Shirley to learn to speak up? It does not. So maybe someday she won't live between the kitchen and the shop. She's not a fool."

I thank you, Papa, for your kindness. It is true about me to this day. I am foolish but I am not a fool.

That night my father kissed me and said with great

59

interest in my career, "Shirley, tomorrow's your big day. Congrats."

"Save it," my mother said. Then she shut all the windows in order to prevent tonsillitis.

In the morning it snowed. On the street corner a tree had been decorated for us by a kind city administration. In order to miss its chilly shadow our neighbors walked three blocks east to buy a loaf of bread. The butcher pulled down black window shades to keep the colored lights from shining on his chickens. Oh, not me. On the way to school, with both my hands I tossed it a kiss of tolerance. Poor thing, it was a stranger in Egypt.

I walked straight into the auditorium past the staring children. "Go ahead, Shirley!" said the monitors. Four boys, big for their age, had already started work as propmen and stagehands.

Mr. Hilton was very nervous. He was not even happy. Whatever he started to say ended in a sideward look of sadness. He sat slumped in the middle of the first row and asked me to help Miss Glacé. I did this, although she thought my voice too resonant and said, "Show-off!"

Parents began to arrive long before we were ready. They wanted to make a good impression. From among the yards of drapes I peeked out at the audience. I saw my embarrassed mother.

Ira, Lester, and Meyer were pasted to their beards by Miss Glacé. She almost forgot to thread the star on its wire, but I reminded her. I coughed a few times to clear my throat. Miss Glacé looked around and saw that everyone was in costume and on line waiting to play his part. She whispered, "All right . . ." Then:

Jackie Sauerfeld, the prettiest boy in first grade,

parted the curtains with his skinny elbow and in a high voice sang out:

> "Parents dear
> We are here
> To make a Christmas play in time.
> It we give
> In narrative
> And illustrate with pantomime."

He disappeared.

My voice burst immediately from the wings to the great shock of Ira, Lester, and Meyer, who were waiting for it but were surprised all the same.

"I remember, I remember, the house where I was born . . ."

Miss Glacé yanked the curtain open and there it was, the house—an old hayloft, where Celia Kornbluh lay in the straw with Cindy Lou, her favorite doll. Ira, Lester, and Meyer moved slowly from the wings toward her, sometimes pointing to a moving star and sometimes ahead to Cindy Lou.

It was a long story and it was a sad story. I carefully pronounced all the words about my lonesome childhood, while little Eddie Braunstein wandered upstage and down with his shepherd's stick, looking for sheep. I brought up lonesomeness again, and not being understood at all except by some women everybody hated. Eddie was too small for that and Marty Groff took his place, wearing his father's prayer shawl. I announced twelve friends, and half the boys in the fourth grade gathered round Marty, who stood on an orange crate while my voice harangued. Sorrowful and loud, I declaimed about love and God and Man, but because of the terrible deceit of Abie Stock we came suddenly to a famous moment. Marty, whose remembering tongue I was, waited at the foot of the cross. He stared desperately at the audience. I groaned, "My God, my God, why hast thou forsaken me?" The soldiers who were sheiks grabbed poor Marty to pin him up to die, but he wrenched free, turned again to the audience, and spread his arms aloft to show despair and the end. I murmured at the top of my voice, "The rest is silence, but as everyone in this room, in this city—in this world—now knows, I shall have life eternal."

That night Mrs. Kornbluh visited our kitchen for a glass of tea.

"How's the virgin?" asked my father with a look of concern.

"For a man with a daughter, you got a fresh mouth, Abramovitch."

"Here," said my father kindly, "have some lemon, it'll sweeten your disposition."

They debated a little in Yiddish, then fell in a puddle of Russian and Polish. What I understood next was my father, who said, "Still and all, it was certainly a beautiful affair, you have to admit, introducing us to the beliefs of a different culture."

"Well, yes," said Mrs. Kornbluh. "The only thing . . . you know Charlie Turner—that cute boy in Celia's class —a couple others? They got very small parts or no part at all. In very bad taste, it seemed to me. After all, it's their religion."

"Ach," explained my mother, "what could Mr. Hilton do? They got very small voices; after all, why should they holler? The English language they know from the beginning by heart. They're blond like angels. You think it's so important they should get in the play? Christmas . . . the whole piece of goods . . . they own it."

I listened and listened until I couldn't listen any more. Too sleepy, I climbed out of bed and kneeled. I made a little church of my hands and said, "Hear, O Israel . . ." Then I called out in Yiddish, "Please, good night, good night. Ssh." My father said, "Ssh yourself," and slammed the kitchen door.

I was happy. I fell asleep at once. I had prayed for everybody: my talking family, cousins far away, passers-by, and all the lonesome Christians. I expected to be heard. My voice was certainly the loudest.

The Contest

Up early or late, it never matters, the day gets away from me. Summer or winter, the shade of trees or their hard shadow, I never get into my Rice Krispies till noon.

I am ambitious, but it's a long-range thing with me. I have my confidential sights on a star, but there's half a lifetime to get to it. Meanwhile I keep my eyes open and am well dressed.

I told the examining psychiatrist for the Army: yes, I like girls. And I do. Not my sister—a pimp's dream. But girls, slim and tender or really stacked, dark brown at their centers, smeared by time. Not my mother, who should've stayed in Freud. I *have* got a sense of humor.

My last girl was Jewish, which is often a warm kind of girl, concerned about food intake and employability. They don't like you to work too hard, I understand, until you're hooked and then, you bastard, sweat!

A medium girl, size twelve, a clay pot with handles— she could be grasped. I met her in the rain outside some cultural activity at Cooper Union or Washington Irving High School. She had no umbrella and I did, so I walked her home to my house. There she remained for several hours, a yawning cavity, half asleep. The rain rained on the ailanthus tree outside my window, the wind rattled the shutters of my old-fashioned window, and I took my time making coffee and carving an ounce of pound cake. I don't believe in force and I would have waited, but her loneliness was very great.

We had quite a nice time for a few weeks. She brought rolls and bagels from wherever the stuff can still be requisitioned. On Sundays she'd come out of Brooklyn with a chicken to roast. She thought I was too skinny. I am, but girls like it. If you're fat, they can see immediately that you'll never need their unique talent for warmth.

Spring came. She said: "Where are we going?" In just those words! Now I have met this attitude before. Apparently, for most women good food and fun for all are too much of a good thing.

The sun absorbed July and she said it again. "Freddy, if we're not going anywhere, I'm not going along any more." We were beach-driven those windy Sundays: her mother must have told her what to say. She said it with such imprisoned conviction.

One Friday night in September I came home from an unlucky party. All the faces had been strange. There were no extra girls, and after some muted conversation with the glorious properties of other men, I felt terrible and went home.

In an armchair, looking at an *Art News* full of Dutchmen who had lived eighty years in forty, was Dorothy. And by her side an overnight case. I could hardly see her face when she stood to greet me, but she made tea first and steamed some of my ardor into the damp night.

"Listen, Freddy," she said. "I told my mother I was visiting Leona in Washington for two days and I fixed it with Leona. Everyone'll cover me"—pouring tea and producing seeded tarts from some secret Flatbush Avenue bakery—all this to change the course of a man's appetite and enable conversation to go forward.

"No, listen, Freddy, you don't take yourself seriously, and that's the reason you can't take anything else—a job, or a—a relationship—seriously. . . . Freddy, you don't listen. You'll laugh, but you're very barbaric. You live at your nerve ends. If you're near a radio, you listen to music; if you're near an open icebox, you stuff yourself; if a girl is within ten feet of you, you have her stripped and on the spit."

"Now, Dotty, don't be so graphic," I said. "Every man is his own rotisserie."

What a nice girl! Say something vulgar and she'd suddenly be all over me, blushing bitterly, glad that the East River separated her from her mother. Poor girl, she was avid.

And she was giving. By Sunday night I had ended half a dozen conversations and nipped their moral judgments at the homiletic root. By Sunday night I had said I love you Dotty, twice. By Monday morning I realized the extent of my commitment and I don't mind saying it prevented my going to a job I had swung on Friday.

My impression of women is that they mean well but are driven to an obsessive end by greedy tradition. When Dot found out that I'd decided against that job (what job? a job, that's all) she took action. She returned my copy of *Nineteen Eighty-four* and said in a note that I could keep the six wineglasses her mother had lent me.

Well, I did miss her; you don't meet such wide-open kindness every day. She was no fool either. I'd say peasant wisdom is what she had. Not too much education. Her hair was long and dark. I had always seen it in neat little coiffures or reparably disarrayed, until that weekend.

It was staggering.

I missed her. And then I didn't have too much luck after that. Very little money to spend, and girls are primordial with intuition. There was one nice little married girl whose husband was puttering around in another postal zone, but her heart wasn't in it. I got some windy copy to do through my brother-in-law, a clean-cut croupier who is always crackling bank notes at family parties. Things picked up.

Out of my gasbag profits one weekend I was propelled into the Craggy-moor, a high-pressure resort, a star-studded haven with eleven hundred acres of golf course. When I returned, exhausted but modest, there she was, right in my parlor-floor front. With a few gasping, kind words and a modern gimmick, she hoped to breathe eternity into a mortal matter, love.

"Ah, Dotty," I said, holding out my accepting arms. "I'm always glad to see you."

Of course she explained. "I didn't come for that really, Freddy. I came to talk to you. We have a terrific chance to make some real money, if you'll only be serious a half hour. You're so clever, and you ought to direct yourself to something. God, you could live in the country. I mean, even if you kept living alone, you could have a decent place on a decent street instead of this dump."

I kissed the tip of her nose. "If you want to be very serious, Dot, let's get out and walk. Come on, get your coat on and tell me all about how to make money."

She did. We walked out to the park and scattered

autumn leaves for an hour. "Now don't laugh, Freddy," she told me. "There's a Yiddish paper called *Morgen-licht*. It's running a contest: JEWS IN THE NEWS. Every day they put in a picture and two descriptions. You have to say who the three people are, add one more fact about them, and then send it in by midnight that night. It runs three months at least."

"A hundred Jews in the news?" I said. "What a tolerant country! So, Dot, what do you get for this useful information?"

"First prize, five thousand dollars and a trip to Israel. Also on return two days each in the three largest European capitals in the Free West."

"Very nice," I said. "What's the idea, though? To uncover the ones that've been passing?"

"Freddy, why do you look at everything inside out? They're just proud of themselves, and they want to make Jews everywhere proud of their contribution to this country. Aren't you proud?"

"Woe to the crown of pride!"

"I don't care what you think. The point is, we know somebody who knows somebody on the paper—he writes a special article once a week—we don't know him really, but our family name is familiar to him. So we have a very good chance if we really do it. Look how smart you are, Freddy. I can't do it myself, Freddy, you have to help me. It's a thing I made up my mind to do anyway. If Dotty Wasserman really makes up her mind, it's practically done."

I hadn't noticed this obstinacy in her character before. I had none in my own. Every weekday night after work she leaned thoughtfully on my desk, wearing for warmth a Harris-tweed jacket that ruined the nap of my arm. Somewhere out of doors a strand of copper in constant agitation carried information from her mother's Brooklyn phone to her ear.

Peering over her shoulder, I would sometimes discover a three-quarter view of a newsworthy Jew or a full view of a half Jew. The fraction did not interfere with the rules. They were glad to extract him and be proud.

The longer we worked the prouder Dotty became. Her face flushed, she'd raise her head from the hieroglyphics and read her own translation: "A gray-headed gentleman very much respected; an intimate of Cabinet members; a true friend to a couple of Presidents; often seen in the park, sitting on a bench."

"Bernard Baruch!" I snapped.

And then a hard one: "Has contributed to the easiness of interstate commerce; his creation is worth millions and was completed last year. Still he has time for Deborah, Susan, Judith, and Nancy, his four daughters."

For this I smoked and guzzled a hot eggnog Dot had whipped up to give me strength and girth. I stared at the stove, the ceiling, my irritable shutters—then I said calmly: "Chaim Pazzi—he's a bridge architect." I never forget a name, no matter what type-face it appears in.

"Imagine it, Freddy. I didn't even know there was a Jew who had such accomplishment in that field."

Actually, it sometimes took as much as an hour to attach a real name to a list of exaggerated attributes. When it took that long I couldn't help muttering, "Well, we've uncovered another one. Put him on the list for Van 2."

Dotty'd say sadly, "I have to believe you're joking."

Well, why do you think she liked me? All you little psychoanalyzed people, now say it at once, in a chorus: "Because she is a masochist and you are a sadist."

No. I was very good to her. And to all the love she gave me, I responded. And I kept all our appointments and called her on Fridays to remind her about Saturday, and when I had money I brought her flowers and once earrings and once a black brassière I saw advertised in the paper with some cleverly stitched windows for ventilation. I still have it. She never dared take it home.

But I will not be eaten by any woman.

My poor old mother died with a sizable chunk of me stuck in her gullet. I was in the Army at the time, but I understand her last words were: "Introduce Freddy to Eleanor Farbstein." Consider the nerve of that woman. Including me in a codicil. She left my sister to that ad man and culinary expert with a crew cut. She left my father to the commiseration of aunts, while me, her prize possession and the best piece of meat in the freezer of her heart, she left to Ellen Farbstein.

As a matter of fact, Dotty said it herself. "I never went with a fellow who paid as much attention as you, Freddy. You're always there. I know if I'm lonesome or depressed all I have to do is call you and you'll meet me downtown and drop whatever you're doing. Don't think I don't appreciate it."

The established truth is, I wasn't doing much. My brother-in-law could have kept me in clover, but he pretended I was a specialist in certain ornate copy infrequently called for by his concern. Therefore I was able to give my wit, energy, and attention to JEWS IN THE NEWS—*Morgenlicht*, the Morning Paper That Comes Out the Night Before.

And so we reached the end. Dot really believed we'd win. I was almost persuaded. Drinking hot chocolate and screwdrivers, we fantasied six weeks away.

We won.

I received a 9 A.M. phone call one midweek morning. "Rise and shine, Frederick P. Sims. We did it. You see, whatever you really try to do, you can do."

She quit work at noon and met me for lunch at an outdoor café in the Village, full of smiles and corrupt with pride. We ate very well and I had to hear the following information—part of it I'd suspected.

It was all in her name. Of course her mother had to get some. She had helped with the translation because Dotty had very little Yiddish actually (not to mention her worry about the security of her old age); and it was necessary, they had decided in midnight conference, to send some money to their old Aunt Lise, who had gotten out of Europe only ninety minutes before it was sealed forever and was now in Toronto among strangers, having lost most of her mind.

The trip abroad to Israel and three other European capitals was for two (2). They had to be married. If our papers could not include one that proved our conjunction by law, she would sail alone. Before I could make my accumulating statement, she shrieked oh! her mother was waiting in front of Lord and Taylor's. And she was off.

I smoked my miserable encrusted pipe and considered my position.

Meanwhile in another part of the city, wheels were

moving, presses humming, and the next day the facts were composed from right to left across the masthead of *Morgenlicht:*

! SNIW NAMRESSAW YTTOD
SREWSNA EHT LLA SWONK LRIG NYLKOORB

Neatly boxed below, a picture of Dot and me eating lunch recalled a bright flash that had illuminated the rice pudding the day before, as I sat drenched in the fizzle of my modest hopes.

I sent Dotty a post card. It said: "No can do."

The final arrangements were complicated due to the reluctance of the Israeli Government to permit egress to dollar bills which were making the grandest tour of all. Once inside that province of cosmopolitans, the dollar was expected to resign its hedonistic role as an American toy and begin the presbyterian life of a tool.

Within two weeks letters came from abroad bearing this information and containing photographs of Dotty smiling at a kibbutz, leaning sympathetically on a wailing wall, unctuous in an orange grove.

I decided to take a permanent job for a couple of months in an agency, attaching the following copy to photographs of upright men!

THIS IS BILL FEARY. HE IS THE MAN WHO WILL TAKE YOUR ORDER FOR —— TONS OF RED LABEL FERTILIZER. HE KNOWS THE MIDWEST. HE KNOWS YOUR NEEDS. CALL HIM BILL AND CALL HIM NOW.

I was neat and brown-eyed, innocent and alert, offended by the chicanery of my fellows, powered by decency, going straight up.

The lean-shanked girls had been brought to New York by tractor and they were going straight up too, through the purgatory of man's avarice to Whore's Heaven, the Palace of Possessions.

While I labored at my dreams, Dotty spent some money to see the leaning tower of Pisa and ride in a gondola. She decided to stay in London at least two weeks because she felt at home there. And so all this profit was at last being left in the hands of foreigners who would invest it to their own advantage.

One misty day the boom of foghorns rolling round Manhattan Island reminded me of a cablegram I had determined to ignore. ARRIVING QUEEN ELIZA-BETH WEDNESDAY 4 P.M. I ignored it successfully all day and was casual with a couple of cool blondes. And went home and was lonely. I was lonely all evening. I tried writing a letter to an athletic girl I'd met in a ski lodge a few weeks before. . . . I thought of calling some friends, but the pure unmentionable fact is that women isolate you. There was no one to call.

I went out for an evening paper. Read it. Listened to the radio. Went out for a morning paper. Had a beer. Read the paper and waited for the calculation of morning.

I never went to work the next day or the day after. No word came from Dot. She must have been crawling with guilt. Poor girl . . .

I finally wrote her a letter. It was very strong.

My dear Dorothy:
When I consider our relationship and recall its seasons, the summer sun that shone on it and the winter

snows it plowed through, I can still find no reason for your unconscionable behavior. I realize that you were motivated by the hideous examples of your mother and all the mothers before her. You were, in a word, a prostitute. The love and friendship I gave were apparently not enough. What did you want? You gave me the swamp waters of your affection to drown in, and because I refused you planned this desperate revenge.

In all earnestness, I helped you, combing my memory for those of our faith who have touched the press-happy nerves of this nation.

What did you want?

Marriage?

Ah, that's it! A happy daddy-and-mommy home. The home-happy day you could put your hair up in curlers, swab cream in the corner of your eyes . . . I'm not sure all this is for Fred.

I am twenty-nine years old and not getting any younger. All around me boy-graduates have attached their bow legs to the Ladder of Success. Dotty Wasserman, Dotty Wasserman, what can I say to you? If you think I have been harsh, face the fact that you haven't dared face me.

We had some wonderful times together. We could have them again. This is a great opportunity to start on a more human basis. You cannot impose your narrow view of life on me. Make up your mind, Dotty Wasserman.

Sincerely with recollected affection,

F.

P.S. This is your *last* chance.

Two weeks later I received a one-hundred-dollar bill.

A week after that at my door I found a carefully packed leather portfolio, hand-sewn in Italy, and a projector with a box of slides showing interesting views of Europe and North Africa.

And after that, nothing at all.

An Interest in Life

My husband gave me a broom one Christmas. This wasn't right. No one can tell me it was meant kindly.

"I don't want you not to have anything for Christmas while I'm away in the Army," he said. "Virginia, please look at it. It comes with this fancy dustpan. It hangs off a stick. Look at it, will you? Are you blind or cross-eyed?"

"Thanks, chum," I said. I had always wanted a dust-pan hooked up that way. It was a good one. My husband doesn't shop in bargain basements or January sales.

Still and all, in spite of the quality, it was a mean present to give a woman you planned on never seeing again, a person you had children with and got onto all the time, drunk or sober, even when everybody had to get up early in the morning.

I asked him if he could wait and join the Army in a half hour, as I had to get the groceries. I don't like to leave kids alone in a three-room apartment full of gas and electricity. Fire may break out from a nasty remark. Or the oldest decides to get even with the youngest.

"Just this once," he said. "But you better figure out how to get along without me."

"You're a handicapped person mentally," I said. "You should've been institutionalized years ago." I slammed

81

the door. I didn't want to see him pack his underwear and ironed shirts.

I never got further than the front stoop, though, because there was Mrs. Raftery, wringing her hands, tears in her eyes as though she had a monopoly on all the good news.

"Mrs. Raftery!" I said, putting my arm around her. "Don't cry." She leaned on me because I am such a horsy build. "Don't cry, Mrs. Raftery, please!" I said.

"That's like you, Virginia. Always looking at the ugly side of things. 'Take in the wash. It's rainin'!' That's you. You're the first one knows it when the dumb-waiter breaks."

"Oh, come on now, that's not so. It just isn't so," I said. "I'm the exact opposite."

"Did you see Mrs. Cullen yet?" she asked, paying no attention.

"Where?"

"Virginia!" she said, shocked. "She's passed away. The whole house knows it. They've got her in white like a bride and you never saw a beautiful creature like that. She must be eighty. Her husband's proud."

"She was never more than an acquaintance; she didn't have any children," I said.

"Well, I don't care about that. Now, Virginia, you do what I say now, you go downstairs and you say like this —listen to me—say, 'I hear, Mr. Cullen, your wife's passed away. I'm sorry.' Then ask him how he is. Then you ought to go around the corner and see her. She's in Witson & Wayde. Then you ought to go over to the church when they carry her over."

"It's not my church," I said.

"That's no reason, Virginia. You go up like this," she said, parting from me to do a prancy dance. "Up the big front steps, into the church you go. It's beautiful in there. You can't help kneeling only for a minute. Then round to the right. Then up the other stairway. Then you come to a great oak door that's arched above you, then," she said, seizing a deep, deep breath, for all the good it would do her, "and then turn the knob slo-owly and open the door and see for yourself: Our Blessed Mother is in charge. Beautiful. Beautiful. Beautiful."

I sighed in and I groaned out, so as to melt a certain pain around my heart. A steel ring like arthritis, at my age.

"You are a groaner," Mrs. Raftery said, gawking into my mouth.

"I am not," I said. I got a whiff of her, a terrible cheap wine lush.

My husband threw a penny at the door from the inside to take my notice from Mrs. Raftery. He rattled the glass door to make sure I looked at him. He had a fat duffel bag on each shoulder. Where did he acquire so much worldly possession? What was in them? My grandma's goose feathers from across the ocean? Or all the diaper-service diapers? To this day the truth is shrouded in mystery.

"What the hell are you doing, Virginia?" he said, dumping them at my feet. "Standing out here on your hind legs telling everybody your business? The Army gives you a certain time, for God's sakes, they're not kidding." Then he said, "I beg your pardon," to Mrs. Raftery. He took hold of me with his two arms as though in love and pressed his body hard against mine so that

I could feel him for the last time and suffer my loss. Then he kissed me in a mean way to nearly split my lip. Then he winked and said, "That's all for now," and skipped off into the future, duffel bags full of rags.

He left me in an embarrassing situation, nearly fainting, in front of that old widow, who can't even remember the half of it. "He's a crock," said Mrs. Raftery. "Is he leaving for good or just temporarily, Virginia?"

"Oh, he's probably deserting me," I said, and sat down on the stoop, pulling my big knees up to my chin.

"If that's the case, tell the Welfare right away," she said. "He's a bum, leaving you just before Christmas. Tell the cops," she said. "They'll provide the toys for the little kids gladly. And don't forget to let the grocer in on it. He won't be so hard on you expecting payment."

She saw that sadness was stretched world-wide across my face. Mrs. Raftery isn't the worst person. She said, "Look around for comfort, dear." With a nervous finger she pointed to the truckers eating lunch on their haunches across the street, leaning on the loading platforms. She waved her hand to include in all the men marching up and down in search of a decent luncheonette. She didn't leave out the six longshoremen loafing under the fish-market marquee. "If their lungs and stomachs ain't crushed by overwork, they disappear somewhere in the world. Don't be disappointed, Virginia. I don't know a man living'd last you a lifetime."

Ten days later Girard asked, "Where's Daddy?"

"Ask me no questions, I'll tell you no lies." I didn't want the children to know the facts. Present or past, a child should have a father.

"Where *is* Daddy?" Girard asked the week after that.

"He joined the Army," I said.

"He made my bunk bed," said Phillip.

"The truth shall make ye free," I said.

Then I sat down with pencil and pad to get in control of my resources. The facts, when I added and subtracted them, were that my husband had left me with fourteen dollars, and the rent unpaid, in an emergency state. He'd claimed he was sorry to do this, but my opinion is, out of sight, out of mind. "The city won't let you starve," he'd said. "After all, you're half the population. You're keeping up the good work. Without you the race would die out. Who'd pay the taxes? Who'd keep the streets clean? There wouldn't be no Army. A man like me wouldn't have no place to go."

I sent Girard right down to Mrs. Raftery with a request about the whereabouts of Welfare. She responded RSVP with an extra comment in left-handed script: "Poor Girard . . . he's never the boy my John was!"

Who asked her?

I called on Welfare right after the new year. In no time I discovered that they're rigged up to deal with liars, and if you're truthful it's disappointing to them. They may even refuse to handle your case if you're too truthful.

They asked sensible questions at first. They asked where my husband had enlisted. I didn't know. They put some letter writers and agents after him. "He's not in the United States Army," they said. "Try the Brazilian Army," I suggested.

They have no sense of kidding around. They're not the least bit lighthearted and they tried. "Oh no," they said. "That was incorrect. He is not in the Brazilian Army."

"No?" I said. "How strange! He must be in the Mexican Navy."

By law, they had to hound his brothers. They wrote to his brother who has a first-class card in the Teamsters and owns an apartment house in California. They asked his two brothers in Jersey to help me. They have large families. Rightfully they laughed. Then they wrote to Thomas, the oldest, the smart one (the one they all worked so hard for years to keep him in college until his brains could pay off). He was the one who sent ten dollars immediately, saying, "What a bastard! I'll send something time to time, Ginny, but whatever you do, don't tell the authorities." Of course I never did. Soon they began to guess they were better people than me, that I was in trouble because I deserved it, and then they liked me better.

But they never fixed my refrigerator. Every time I called I said patiently, "The milk is sour . . ." I said, "Corn beef went bad." Sitting in that beer-stinking phone booth in Felan's for the sixth time (sixty cents) with the baby on my lap and Barbie tapping at the glass door with an American flag, I cried into the secretary's hardhearted ear, "I bought real butter for the holiday, and it's rancid . . ." They said, "You'll have to get a better bid on the repair job."

While I waited indoors for a man to bid, Girard took to swinging back and forth on top of the bathroom door, just to soothe himself, giving me the laugh, dreamy, nibbling calcimine off the ceiling. On first sight Mrs. Raftery said, "Whack the monkey, he'd be better off on arsenic."

But Girard is my son and I'm the judge. It means a terrible thing for the future, though I don't know what to call it.

It was from constantly thinking of my foreknowledge on this and other subjects, it was from observing when I put my lipstick on daily, how my face was just curling up to die, that John Raftery came from Jersey to rescue me.

On Thursdays, anyway, John Raftery took the tubes in to visit his mother. The whole house knew it. She was cheerful even before breakfast. She sang out loud in a girlish brogue that only came to tongue for grand occasions. Hanging out the wash, she blushed to recall what a remarkable boy her John had been. "Ask the sisters around the corner," she said to the open kitchen windows. "They'll never forget John."

That particular night after supper Mrs. Raftery said to her son, "John, how come you don't say hello to your old friend Virginia? She's had hard luck and she's gloomy."

"Is that so, Mother?" he said, and immediately climbed two flights to knock at my door.

"Oh, John," I said at the sight of him, hat in hand in a white shirt and blue-striped tie, spick-and-span, a Sunday-school man. "Hello!"

"Welcome, John!" I said. "Sit down. Come right in. How are you? You look awfully good. You do. Tell me, how've you been all this time, John?"

"How've I been?" he asked thoughtfully. To answer within reason, he described his life with Margaret, marriage, work, and children up to the present day.

I had nothing good to report. Now that he had put the

subject around before my very eyes, every burnt-up day of my life smoked in shame, and I couldn't even get a clear view of the good half hours.

"Of course," he said, "you do have lovely children. Noticeable-looking, Virginia. Good looks is always something to be thankful for."

"Thankful?" I said. "I don't have to thank anything but my own foolishness for four children when I'm twenty-six years old, deserted, and poverty-struck, regardless of looks. A man can't help it, but I could have behaved better."

"Don't be so cruel on yourself, Ginny," he said. "Children come from God."

"You're still great on holy subjects, aren't you? You know damn well where children come from."

He did know. His red face reddened further. John Raftery has had that color coming out on him boy and man from keeping his rages so inward.

Still he made more sense in his conversation after that, and I poured fresh tea to tell him how my husband used to like me because I was a passionate person. That was until he took a look around and saw how in the long run this life only meant more of the same thing. He tried to turn away from me once he came to this understanding, and make me hate him. His face changed. He gave up his brand of cigarettes, which we had in common. He threw out the two pairs of socks I knitted by hand. "If there's anything I hate in this world, it's navy blue," he said. Oh, I could have dyed them. I would have done anything for him, if he were only not too sorry to ask me.

"You were a nice kid in those days," said John, referring to certain Saturday nights. "A wild, nice kid."

"Aaah," I said, disgusted. Whatever I was then, was on the way to where I am now. "I was fresh. If I had a kid like me, I'd slap her cross-eyed."

The very next Thursday John gave me a beautiful radio with a record player. "Enjoy yourself," he said. That really made Welfare speechless. We didn't own any records, but the investigator saw my burden was lightened and he scribbled a dozen pages about it in his notebook.

On the third Thursday he brought a walking doll (twenty-four inches) for Linda and Barbie with a card inscribed, "A baby doll for a couple of dolls." He had also had a couple of drinks at his mother's, and this made him want to dance. "La-la-la," he sang, a ramrod swaying in my kitchen chair. "La-la-la, let yourself go . . ."

"You gotta give a little," he sang, "live a little . . ." He said, "Virginia, may I have this dance?"

"Sssh, we finally got them asleep. Please, turn the radio down. Quiet. Deathly silence, John Raftery."

"Let me do your dishes, Virginia."

"Don't be silly, you're a guest in my house," I said. "I still regard you as a guest."

"I want to do something for you, Virginia."

"Tell me I'm the most gorgeous thing," I said, dipping my arm to the funny bone in dish soup.

He didn't answer. "I'm having a lot of trouble at work," was all he said. Then I heard him push the chair back. He came up behind me, put his arms around my waistline, and kissed my cheek. He whirled me around and took my hands. He said, "An old friend is better than rubies." He looked me in the eye. He held my attention by trying to be honest. And he kissed me a short sweet kiss on my mouth.

"Please sit down, Virginia," he said. He kneeled before me and put his head in my lap. I was stirred by so much activity. Then he looked up at me and, as though proposing marriage for life, he offered—because he was drunk—to place his immortal soul in peril to comfort me.

First I said, "Thank you." Then I said, "No."

I was sorry for him, but he's devout, a leader of the Fathers' Club at his church, active in all the lay groups for charities, orphans, etc. I knew that if he stayed late to love with me, he would not do it lightly but would in the end pay terrible penance and ruin his long life. The responsibility would be on me.

So I said no.

And Barbie is such a light sleeper. All she has to do, I thought, is wake up and wander in and see her mother and her new friend John with his pants around his knees, wrestling on the kitchen table. A vision like that could affect a kid for life.

I said no.

Everyone in this building is so goddamn nosy. That evening I had to say no.

But John came to visit, anyway, on the fourth Thursday. This time he brought the discarded dresses of Margaret's daughters, organdy party dresses and glazed cotton for every day. He gently admired Barbara and Linda, his blue eyes rolling to back up a couple of dozen oohs and ahs.

Even Phillip, who thinks God gave him just a certain number of hellos and he better save them for the final judgment, Phillip leaned on John and said, "Why don't you bring your boy to play with me? I don't have nobody who to play with." (Phillip's a liar. There must be at least seventy-one children in this house, pale pink to medium brown, English-talking and gibbering in Spanish, rough-and-tough boys, the Lone Ranger's bloody pals, or the exact picture of Supermouse. If a boy wanted a friend, he could pick the very one out of his neighbors.

Also, Girard is a cold fish. He was in a lonesome despair. Sometimes he looked in the mirror and said, "How come I have such an ugly face? My nose is funny. Mostly people don't like me." He was a liar too. Girard has a face like his father's. His eyes are the color of those little blue plums in August. He looks like an advertisement in a magazine. He could be a child model and make a lot of money. He is my first child, and if he thinks he is ugly, I think I am ugly.

John said, "I can't stand to see a boy mope like that. . . . What do the sisters say in school?"

"He doesn't pay attention is all they say. You can't get much out of them."

"My middle boy was like that," said John. "Couldn't take an interest. Aaah, I wish I didn't have all that headache on the job. I'd grab Girard by the collar and make him take notice of the world. I wish I could ask him out to Jersey to play in all that space."

"Why not?" I said.

"Why, Virginia, I'm surprised you don't know why not. You know I can't take your children out to meet my children."

I felt a lot of strong arthritis in my ribs.

"My mother's the funny one, Virginia." He felt he had to continue with the subject matter. "I don't know. I

91

guess she likes the idea of bugging Margaret. She says, 'You goin' up, John?' 'Yes, Mother,' I say. 'Behave yourself, John,' she says. 'That husband might come home and hack-saw you into hell. You're a Catholic man, John,' she says. But I figured it out. She likes to know I'm in the building. I swear, Virginia, she wishes me the best of luck."

"I do too, John," I said. We drank a last glass of beer to make sure of a peaceful sleep. "Good night, Virginia," he said, looping his muffler neatly under his chin. "Don't worry. I'll be thinking of what to do about Girard."

I got into the big bed that I share with the girls in the little room. For once I had no trouble falling asleep. I only had to worry about Linda and Barbara and Phillip. It was a great relief to me that John had taken over the thinking about Girard.

John was sincere. That's true. He paid a lot of attention to Girard, smoking out all his sneaky sorrows. He registered him into a wild pack of cub scouts that went up to the Bronx once a week to let off steam. He gave him a Junior Erector Set. And sometimes when his family wasn't listening he prayed at great length for him.

One Sunday, Sister Veronica said in her sweet voice from another life, "He's not worse. He might even be a little better. How are *you*, Virginia?" putting her hand on mine. Everybody around here acts like they know everything.

"Just fine," I said.

"We ought to start on Phillip," John said, "if it's true Girard's improving."

"You should've been a social worker, John."

"A lot of people have noticed that about me," said John.

"Your mother was always acting so crazy about you, how come she didn't knock herself out a little to see you in college? Like we did for Thomas?"

"Now, Virginia, be fair. She's a poor old woman. My father was a weak earner. She had to have my wages, and I'll tell you, Virginia, I'm not sorry. Look at Thomas. He's still in school. Drop him in this jungle and he'd be devoured. He hasn't had a touch of real life. And here I am with a good chunk of a family, a home of my own, a name in the building trades. One thing I have to tell you, the poor old woman is sorry. I said one day (oh, in passing—years ago) that I might marry you. She stuck a knife in herself. It's a fact. Not more than an eighth of an inch. You never saw such a gory Sunday. One thing —you would have been a better daughter-in-law to her than Margaret."

"Marry me?" I said.

"Well, yes. . . . Aaah—I always liked you, then . . . Why do you think I'd sit in the shade of this kitchen every Thursday night? For God's sakes, the only warm thing around here is this teacup. Yes, sir, I did want to marry you, Virginia."

"No kidding, John? Really?" It was nice to know. Better late than never, to learn you were desired in youth.

I didn't tell John, but the truth is, I would never have married him. Once I met my husband with his winking looks, he was my only interest. Wild as I had been with John and others, I turned all my wildness over to him and then there was no question in my mind.

Still, face facts, if my husband didn't budge on in life,

it was my fault. On me, as they say, be it. I greeted the morn with a song. I had a hello for everyone but the landlord. Ask the people on the block, come or go—even the Spanish ones, with their sad dark faces—they have to smile when they see me.

But for his own comfort, he should have done better lifewise and moneywise. I was happy, but I am now in possession of knowledge that this is wrong. Happiness isn't so bad for a woman. She gets fatter, she gets older, she could lie down, nuzzling a regiment of men and little kids, she could just die of the pleasure. But men are different, they have to own money, or they have to be famous, or everybody on the block has to look up to them from the cellar stairs.

A woman counts her children and acts snotty, like she invented life, but men *must* do well in the world. I know that men are not fooled by being happy.

"A funny guy," said John, guessing where my thoughts had gone. "What stopped him up? He was nobody's fool. He had a funny thing about him, Virginia, if you don't mind my saying so. He wasn't much distance up, but he was all set and ready to be looking down on us all."

"He was very smart, John. You don't realize that. His hobby was crossword puzzles, and I said to him real often, as did others around here, that he ought to go out on the '$64 Question.' Why not? But he laughed. You know what he said? He said, 'That proves how dumb you are if you think I'm smart.'"

"A funny guy," said John. "Get it all off your chest," he said. "Talk it out, Virginia; it's the only way to kill the pain."

By and large, I was happy to oblige. Still I could not carry through about certain cruel remarks. It was like trying to move back into the dry mouth of a nightmare to remember that the last day I was happy was the middle of a week in March, when I told my husband I was going to have Linda. Barbara was five months old to the hour. The boys were three and four. I had to tell him. It was the last day with anything happy about it.

Later on he said, "Oh, you make me so sick, you're so goddamn big and fat, you look like a goddamn brownstone, the way you're squared off in front."

"Well, where are you going tonight?" I asked.

"How should I know?" he said. "Your big ass takes up the whole goddamn bed," he said. "There's no room for me." He bought a sleeping bag and slept on the floor.

I couldn't believe it. I would start every morning fresh. I couldn't believe that he would turn against me so, while I was still young and even his friends still liked me.

But he did, he turned absolutely against me and became no friend of mine. "All you ever think about is making babies. This place stinks like the men's room in the BMT. It's a fucking *pissoir*." He was strong on truth all through the year. "That kid eats more than the five of us put together," he said. "Stop stuffing your face, you fat dumbbell," he said to Phillip.

Then he worked on the neighbors. "Get that nosy old bag out of here," he said. "If she comes on once more with 'my son in the building trades' I'll squash her for the cat."

Then he turned on Spielvogel, the checker, his oldest friend, who only visited on holidays and never spoke to

me (shy, the way some bachelors are). "That sonofabitch, don't hand me that friendship crap, all he's after
is your ass. That's what I need—a little shitmaker of his
using up the air in this flat."

And then there was no one else to dispose of. We were
left alone fair and square, facing each other.

"Now, Virginia," he said, "I come to the end of my
rope. I see a black wall ahead of me. What the hell am I
supposed to do? I only got one life. Should I lie down
and die? I don't know what to do any more. I'll give it
to you straight, Virginia, if I stick around, you can't help
it, you'll hate me . . ."

"I hate you right now," I said. "So do whatever you
like."

"This place drives me nuts," he mumbled. "I don't
know what to do around here. I want to get you a present. Something."

"I told you, do whatever you like. Buy me a rattrap
for rats."

That's when he went down to the House Appliance
Store, and he brought back a new broom and a classy
dustpan.

"A new broom sweeps clean," he said. "I got to get
out of here," he said. "I'm going nuts." Then he began
to stuff the duffel bags, and I went to the grocery store
but was stopped by Mrs. Raftery, who had to tell me
what she considered so beautiful—death—then he kissed
and went to join some army somewhere.

I didn't tell John any of this, because I think it makes
a woman look too bad to tell on how another man has
treated her. He begins to see her through the other man's
eyes, a sitting duck, a skinful of flaws. After all, I had

come to depend on John. All my husband's friends were strangers now, though I had always said to them, "Feel welcome."

And the family men in the building looked too cunning, as though they had all personally deserted me. If they met me on the stairs, they carried the heaviest groceries up and helped bring Linda's stroller down, but they never asked me a question worth answering at all.

Besides that, Girard and Phillip taught the girls the days of the week: Monday, Tuesday, Wednesday, Johnday, Friday. They waited for him once a week, under the hallway lamp, half asleep like bugs in the sun, sitting in their little chairs with their names on in gold, a birth present from my mother-in-law. At fifteen after eight he punctually came, to read a story, pass out some kisses, and tuck them into bed.

But one night, after a long Johnday of them squealing my eardrum split, after a rainy afternoon with brother constantly raising up his hand against brother, with the girls near ready to go to court over the proper ownership of Melinda Lee, the twenty-four-inch walking doll, the doorbell rang three times. Not any of those times did John's face greet me.

I was too ashamed to call down to Mrs. Raftery, and she was too mean to knock on my door and explain.

He didn't come the following Thursday either. Girard said sadly, "He must've run away, John."

I had to give him up after two weeks' absence and no word. I didn't know how to tell the children: something about right and wrong, goodness and meanness, men and women. I had it all at my finger tips, ready to hand over. But I didn't think I ought to take mistakes and truth away from them. Who knows? They might make a truer friend in this world somewhere than I have ever made. So I just put them to bed and sat in the kitchen and cried.

In the middle of my third beer, searching in my mind for the next step, I found the decision to go on "Strike It Rich." I scrounged some paper and pencil from the toy box and I listed all my troubles, which must be done in order to qualify. The list when complete could have brought tears to the eye of God if He had a minute. At the sight of it my bitterness began to improve. All that is really necessary for survival of the fittest, it seems, is an interest in life, good, bad, or peculiar.

As always happens in these cases where you have begun to help yourself with plans, news comes from an opposite direction. The doorbell rang, two short and two long—meaning John.

My first thought was to wake the children and make them happy. "No! No!" he said. "Please don't put yourself to that trouble. Virginia, I'm dog-tired," he said. "Dog-tired. My job is a damn headache. It's too much. It's all day and it scuttles my mind at night, and in the end who does the credit go to?

"Virginia," he said, "I don't know if I can come any more. I've been wanting to tell you. I just don't know. What's it all about? Could you answer me if I asked you? I can't figure this whole thing out at all."

I started the tea steeping because his fingers when I touched them were cold. I didn't speak. I tried looking at it from his man point of view, and I thought he had to take a bus, the tubes, and a subway to see me; and then the subway, the tubes, and a bus to go back home at

1 A.M. It wouldn't be any trouble at all for him to part with us forever. I thought about my life, and I gave strongest consideration to my children. If given the choice, I decided to choose not to live without him.

"What's that?" he asked, pointing to my careful list of troubles. "Writing a letter?"

"Oh no," I said, "it's for 'Strike It Rich.' I hope to go on the program."

"Virginia, for goodness' sakes," he said, giving it a glance, "you don't have a ghost. They'd laugh you out of the studio. Those people really suffer."

"Are you sure, John?" I asked.

"No question in my mind at all," said John. "Have you ever seen that program? I mean, in addition to all of this—the little disturbances of man"—he waved a scornful hand at my list—"they *suffer*. They live in the forefront of tornadoes, their lives are washed off by floods—catastrophes of God. Oh, Virginia."

"Are you sure, John?"

"For goodness' sake . . ."

Sadly I put my list away. Still, if things got worse, I could always make use of it.

Once that was settled, I acted on an earlier decision. I pushed his cup of scalding tea aside. I wedged myself onto his lap between his hard belt buckle and the table. I put my arms around his neck and said, "How come you're so cold, John?" He has a kind face and he knew how to look astonished. He said, "Why, Virginia, I'm getting warmer." We laughed.

John became a lover to me that night.

Mrs. Raftery is sometimes silly and sick from her private source of cheap wine. She expects John often.

"Honor your mother, what's the matter with you, John?" she complains. "Honor. Honor."

"Virginia dear," she says. "You never would've taken John away to Jersey like Margaret. I wish he'd've married you."

"You didn't like me much in those days."

"That's a lie," she says. I know she's a hypocrite, but no more than the rest of the world.

What is remarkable to me is that it doesn't seem to conscience John as I thought it might. It is still hard to believe that a man who sends out the Ten Commandments every year for a Christmas card can be so easy buttoning and unbuttoning.

Of course we must be very careful not to wake the children or disturb the neighbors who will enjoy another person's excitement just so far, and then the pleasure enrages them. We must be very careful for ourselves too, for when my husband comes back, realizing the babies are in school and everything easier, he won't forgive me if I've started it all up again—noisy signs of life that are so much trouble to a man.

We haven't seen him in two and a half years. Although people have suggested it, I do not want the police or Intelligence or a private eye or anyone to go after him to bring him back. I know that if he expected to stay away forever he would have written and said so. As it is, I just don't know what evening, any time, he may appear. Sometimes, stumbling over a blockbuster of a dream at midnight, I wake up to vision his soft arrival.

He comes in the door with his old key. He gives me a strict look and says, "Well, you look older, Virginia." "So do you," I say, although he hasn't changed a bit.

He settles in the kitchen because the children are asleep all over the rest of the house. I unknot his tie and offer him a cold sandwich. He raps my backside, paying attention to the bounce. I walk around him as though he were a Maypole, kissing as I go.

"I didn't like the Army much," he says. "Next time I think I might go join the Merchant Marine."

"What army?" I say.

"It's pretty much the same everywhere," he says.

"I wouldn't be a bit surprised," I say.

"I lost my cuff link, goddamnit," he says, and drops to the floor to look for it. I go down too on my knees, but I know he never had a cuff link in his life. Still I would do a lot for him.

"Got you off your feet that time," he says, laughing. "Oh yes, I did." And before I can even make myself half comfortable on that polka-dotted linoleum, he got onto me right where we were, and the truth is, we were so happy, we forgot the precautions.

An Irrevocable Diameter

One day in August, in a quiet little suburb hot with cars and zoned for parks, I, Charles C. Charley, met a girl named Cindy. There were lots of Cindys strolling in the woods that afternoon, but mine was a real citizen with yellow hair that never curled (it hung). When I came across her, she had left the woods to lie around her father's attic. She rested on an army cot, her head on no pillow, smoking a cigarette that stood straight up, a dreamy funnel. Ashes fell gently to her chest, which was relatively new, covered by dacron and Egyptian cotton, and waiting to be popular.

I had just installed an air conditioner, 20 per cent off and late in the season. That's how I make a living. I bring ease to noxious kitchens and fuming bedrooms. People who have tried to live by cross ventilation alone have thanked me.

On the first floor the system was in working order, absolutely perfect and guaranteed. Upstairs, under a low unfinished ceiling, that Cindy lay in the deadest center of an August day. Her forehead was damp, mouth slightly open between drags, a furious and sweaty face, hardly made up except around the eyes, but certainly cared for, cheeks scrubbed and eyebrows brushed, a lifetime's deposit of vitamins, the shiny daughter of cash in the bank.

"Aren't you hot?" I inquired.

"Boiling," she said.

"Why stay up here?" I asked like a good joe.

"That's my business," she said.

"Ah, come on, little one," I said, "don't be grouchy."

"What's it to you?" she asked.

I took her cigarette and killed it between forefinger and thumb. Then she looked at me and saw me for what I was, not an ordinary union brother but a perfectly comfortable way to spend five minutes.

"What's your name?" she asked.

"Charles," I said.

"Is this your business? Are you the boss?"

"I am," I said.

"Listen, Charles, when you were in high school, did *you* know exactly what your interests were?"

"Yes," I said. "Girls."

She turned over on her side so we could really talk this out head on. I stooped to meet her. She smiled. "Charles, I'm almost finished with school and I can't even decide what to take in college. I don't really want to be anything. I don't know what to do," she said. "What do you think I should do?"

I gave her a serious answer, a handful of wisdom. "In the first place, don't let them shove. Who do they think they're kidding? Most people wouldn't know if they had a million years what they wanted to be. They just sort of become."

She raised a golden brow. "Do you think so, Charles? Are you sure? Listen, how old are *you*?"

"Thirty-two," I said as quick as nighttime in the tropics. "Thirty-two," I repeated to reassure myself, since I

106

was subtracting three years wasted in the Army as well as the first two years of my life, which I can't remember a damn thing about anyway.

"You seem older."

"Isn't thirty-two old enough? Is it too old?"

"Oh no, Charles, I don't like kids. I mean they're mostly boring. They don't have a remark to make on anything worth listening to. They think they're the greatest. They don't even dance very well."

She fell back, her arms swinging on either side of the cot. She stared at the ceiling. "If you want to know something," she said, "they don't even know how to kiss."

Then lightly on the very tip of her nose, I, Charles C. Charley, kissed her once and, if it may be sworn, in jest.

To this she replied, "Are you married, by any chance?"

"No," I said, "are you?"

"Oh, Charles," she said, "how could I be married? I haven't even graduated yet."

"You must be a junior," I said, licking my lips.

"Oh, Charles," she said, "that's what I mean. If you were a kid like Mike or Sully or someone, you'd go crazy. Whenever they kiss me, you'd think their whole life was going to change. Honestly, Charles, they lose their breath, they sneeze—just when you're getting in the mood. They stop in the middle to tell you a dirty joke."

"Imagine that!" I said. "How about trying someone over sixteen?"

"Don't fish," she said in a peaceful, happy way. "Anyway, talk very low. In fact, whisper. If my father comes home and hears me even mention kissing, he'll kill us both."

I laughed. My little factories of admiration had started to hum and I missed her meaning.

What I observed was the way everything about this Cindy was new and unused. Her parts, visible or wrapped, were tooled for display. All the exaggerated bones of childhood and old age were bedded down in a cozy consistency of girl.

I offered her another cigarette. I stood up and, ducking the rafters, walked back and forth alongside the cot. She held her fresh cigarette aloft and crossed her eyes at it. Ashes fell, little fine feathers. I leaned forward until I was close enough for comfort. I blew them all away.

I thought of praying for divine guidance in line with the great spiritual renaissance of our time. But I am all thumbs in that kind of deciduous conversation. I asked myself, did I, as God's creature under the stars, have the right to evade an event, a factual occurrence, to parry an experience or even a small peradventure?

I relit her cigarette. Then I said, with no pacing at all, like a person who lacks aptitude, "What do you think, Cindy, listen, will you have trouble with your family about dating me? I'd like to spend a nice long evening with you. I haven't talked to someone your age in a long time. Or we could go swimming, dancing, I don't know. I don't want you to have any trouble, though. Would it help if *I* asked your mother? Do you think she'd let you?"

"That'll be the day," she said. "No one tells *me* who to go out with. No one. I've got a new bathing suit, Charles. I'd love to go."

"I bet you look like a potato sack in it."

"Oh, Charley, quit kidding."

"O.K.," I said. "But don't call me Charley. Charley is my last name. Charles is my first. There's a 'C' in the middle. Charles C. Charley is who I am."

"O.K.," she said. "My name is Cindy."

"I know that," I said.

Then I said goodbye and left her nearly drowned in perspiration, still prone, smoking another cigarette, and staring dreamily at a beam from which hung an old doll's house with four upstairs bedrooms.

Outside I made lighthearted obeisance to the entire household, from rumpus room to expanding attic. I hopped onto my three-wheeled scooter and went forward on spectacular errands of mercy across the sycamore-studded seat of this fat county.

At 4 A.M. of the following Saturday morning I delivered Cindy to her eight-room house with two and a half bathrooms. Mrs. Graham was waiting. She didn't look at me at all. She began to cry. She sniffed and stopped crying. "Cindy, it's so late. Daddy went to the police. We were frightened about you. He went to see the lieutenant." Then she waited, forlorn. Before her very eyes the friend she had been raising for years, the rejuvenating confidante, had deserted her. I was sorry. I thought Cindy ought to get her a cold drink. I wanted to say, "Don't worry, Mrs. Graham. I didn't knock the kid up."

But Cindy burned. "I am just sick of this crap!" she yelled. "I am heartily and utterly sick of being pushed around. Every time I come home a little late, you call the police. This is the third time, the third time. I am sick of you and Daddy. I hate this place. I hate living here. I told you last year. I hate it here. I'm sick of this place and the phony trains and no buses and I can't drive. I hate the kids around here. They're all dopes. You follow me around. I hate the two of you. I wish I was in China." She stamped her feet three times, then ran up to her room.

In this way she avoided her father, who came growling past me where I still stood in the doorway. I was comforting Mrs. Graham. "You know adolescence is a very difficult period . . ." But he interrupted. He looked over his shoulder, saw it was really me, and turned like a man to say it to my face. "You sonofabitch, where the hell were you?"

"Nothing to worry about, Mr. Graham. We just took a boat ride."

"You'd better call the police and tell them Cindy's home, Alvin," said Mrs. Graham.

"Where to?" he said. "Greenwich Village?"

"No, no," I said reasonably. "I took Cindy out to Pottsburg—it's one of those amusement parks there on the other side of the harbor. It's a two-hour ride. There's dancing on the boat. We missed a boat and had to wait two more hours, and then we missed the train."

"This boat goes straight to Pottsburg?"

"Oh yes," I said.

"Alvin," said Mrs. Graham, "please call the police. They'll be all over town."

"O.K., O.K.," he said. "Where's Cynthy Anne?"

"Asleep probably," Mrs. Graham said. "Please, Alvin."

"O.K., O.K.," he said. "You go up too, Ellie. Go on,

don't argue. Go on up and go to sleep. I want to talk to Mr. What's-His-Name for a couple of minutes. Go on now, Ellie, before I get sore.

"Now, you!" he said, turning to me. "Let's go into my den." He pointed to it with a meaty shoulder. I went before him.

I could not really see him through the 4 A.M. haze, but I got the outlines. He was a big guy with a few years on me, a little more money, status, and enough community standing to freeze him where he stood. All he could do was bellow like a bull in his own parlor, crinolines cracking all around him.

"You know, sonny," he said, leaning forward in a friendly way, "if you don't keep away from my kid—in fact, if I ever see you with her again—I'm gonna bring this knee right up"—pointing to it—"and let you have it."

"What did *I* do?"

"You didn't do anything and you're not going to. Stay away. . . . Listen," he said intimately, man to man. "What good is she? She's only a kid. She isn't even sure which end is up."

I looked to see if he really believed that. From the relaxed condition of his face and the sincere look in his eyes, I had to say to myself, yes, that's what he believes.

"Mr. Graham," I said, "I called for Cindy at her own door. Your wife met me. I did not come sneaking around."

"Don't give me any crap," he said.

"Well, all right, Mr. Graham," I said. "I'm the last guy to create a situation. What do you want me to do?"

"I don't want you near this place."

I pretended to give it some thought. But my course

was clear. I had to sleep two hours before morning at least. "I'll tell you what, Mr. Graham. I'm the last guy to create a situation. I just won't see Cindy any more. But there's something we ought to do—from her point of view. The hell with me . . ."

"The hell with you is right," he said. "What?"

"I think a little note's in order, a little letter explaining about all this. I don't want her to think I hate her. You got to watch out with kids that age. They're sensitive. I'd like to write to her."

"O.K.," he said. "That's a good idea, Charley. You do that little thing, and as far as I'm concerned we can call it square. I know how it is in the outfield, boy. Cold. I don't blame you for trying. But this kid's got a family to watch out for her. And I'll tell you another thing. I'm the kind of father, I'm not ashamed to beat the shit out of her if I have to, and the *Ladies' Home Journal* can cry in their soda pop, for all I care. O.K.?" he asked, standing up to conclude. "Everything O.K.?

"I'm dying on my dogs," he said in a kindlier tone. Then in a last snarl at the passing stranger he said, "But you better not try this neighborhood again."

"Well, so long," I said, hopefully passing out of his life. "Don't take any woolen condoms." But when he cantered out to look for me, I was gone.

Two days later I was sitting peacefully in my little office, which is shaded by a dying sycamore. I had three signed-for, cash-on-delivery jobs ahead of me, and if I weren't a relaxed guy I would have been out cramming my just rewards. I was reading a little book called *Medieval People*, which I enjoyed because I am interested in man as a person. It's a hobby. (I should have been a psychologist. I have an ear.) I was eating a hero sandwich. Above my head was a sign in gold which declared AERI AIR CONDITIONERS. Up the Aeri Mountain, Down the Rushing Glen, Aeri Goes Wherever, Man Builds Homes for Men.

The telephone gave its half-turned-off buzz. It was Cindy, to whom I offered a joyous hello, but she was crying. She said three times, "Oh, I'm sorry. Oh, I'm sorry. Oh, I'm sorry."

"I am too, honey." I thought of how to console her. "But you know there's some justice to it. Your daddy's really planning a lovely future for you."

"No, Charles, that's not it. You don't know what happened. Charles, it's terrible. It's all my fault; he's going to put you in jail. But he got me so mad . . . It's my fault, Charles. He's crazy, he really means it."

On the pale reflection in the colorless window glass, I blanched. "O.K.," I said. "Don't cry any more. Tell me the truth."

"Oh, Charles . . ." she said. Then she described the events of the previous evening. Here they are. I have taken them right out of Cindy's mouth.

"Cindy," Mr. Graham said, "I don't want you to go around with a man like that—old enough to be your father almost."

"Oh, for godsakes, Daddy, he's very nice. He's a wonderful dancer."

"I don't like it, Cindy. Not at all. I don't even like your dancing with him. There are a lot of things you don't know about people and things, Cindy. I don't like you dancing with him. I don't approve of a man of that age even putting his arm around a teen-ager like you. You know I want the best for you, Cindy Anne. I want you to have a full and successful life. Keeping up your friendship with him, even if it's as innocent and pleasant as you claim, would be a real hindrance. I want you to go away to school and have a wonderful time with fellows your own age, dancing with them, and, you know, you might fall in love or something. . . . I'm not so stupid and blind. You know, I was young once too."

"Oh, Daddy, there's still plenty of life in you, for goodness' sakes."

"I hope so, Cindy. But what I want to tell you, honey, is that I've asked this man Charles to please stay away from you and write you a nice letter and he agreed, because, after all, you are a very pretty girl and people can often be tempted to do things they don't want to do, no matter how nice they are."

"You asked him to stay away?"

"Yes."

"And he agreed?"

"Yes, he did."

"Did he say he might be tempted?"

"Well . . ."

"Did he say he *might* be tempted?"

"Well, actually, he said he . . ."

"He just agreed? He didn't even get *angry*? He didn't even *want* to see me again?"

"He'll write you, honey."

"He'll write me? Did he say he'll write me? That's all? Who does he think I am? An idiot? A dope? A little nitwit from West Main Street? Where does he get off?

That fat slob . . . What does he think I am? Didn't he even *want* to see me again? He's gonna write me?"

"Cindy!"

"That's all? That's what he wanted me for? He's gonna write me a letter? Daddy . . . Daddy . . ."

"Cindy! What happened last night?"

"Why do you go stick your nose in my business? Doesn't anything ever happen to you? I was just getting along fine for five minutes. Why do you always sit around the house with your nose in my business?"

"Cindy, were you fooling around with that man?"

"Why can't you leave me alone for five minutes? Doesn't anyone else want you around any more someplace? What do you want from me?"

"Cindy." He gripped her wrist. "Cindy! Answer me this minute. Were you?"

"Stop yelling. I'm not deaf."

"Cindy, were you fooling around with that man? Answer!"

"Leave me alone," she cried. "Just leave me alone."

"You answer me this minute," he shouted.

"I'll answer you, all right," she said. "I was not fooling around. I was not fooling. You asked me. I was not fooling. I went upstairs where the lifeboat is and I lay down right underneath it and I did it with Charles."

"What did you do?" gasped her father.

"And I ruined my blue dress," she screamed. "And you're so dumb you didn't even know it."

"Your blue dress?" he asked, scarcely breathing to hear the answer. "Cindy Anne, why?"

"Because I wanted to. I wanted to."

"What?" he asked dimly.

"I wanted to, Daddy," she said.

"Oh, my God!" he said. "My God, my God, what did I do?"

Half an hour later Mrs. Graham returned loaded with goodies from the KrissKross Shopping Center. Cindy was crying in the kitchen, and in the TV room Mr. Graham sat in his red leatherette, eyes closed, his pale lips whispered, "It's statutory rape. . . . It's transporting a minor . . ."

Cindy, my little pal, came lolling down the courtroom aisle with a big red smile, friend to the entire court. She wiggled a little in order to convey the notion that she was really a juvenile whore and I was not accountable. Nobody believed her. She was obviously only the singed daughter of a Campfire Girl.

Besides—philosophically and with a heavy hand—I had decided my fate was written. O.K., O.K., O.K., I said to the world and, staring inward, I overcame my incarceration anxiety. If a period of self-revelation under spartan circumstances was indicated, I was willing to accept the fact that this mysterious move of His might be meant to perform wonders. (Nehru, I understand, composed most of his books in jail.) Do not assume any particular religiosity in me. I have no indoctrinated notion about what He is like: size, shape, or high I.Q.

Adjustments aside, I was embarrassed by the sudden appearance of my mother, who had been hounded from home by the local papers. She sat as close to me as the courtroom design would allow and muttered when apropos, "She's a tramp," or "You're an idiot." Once we were allowed to speak to each other: she said, "What a wild Indian you turned into, Charles."

Was she kidding? Was she proud? Why did she even care? Me, Charles C. Charley, puffed and scared, I am not the baby who lay suffocating under her left tit. I am not the boy who waited for her every night at the factory gate. I am not even any more the draftee who sent her portable pieces of an Italian church.

"What kind of a boy was your son?" my stupid lawyer asked. She peered at him, her fat face the soundboard of silence. "I said, Mrs. Charley, what kind of a boy was your son?"

After a few disengaged moments she replied, "I don't know much about any of my boys; they're a surprise to me." Then her lips met and her hands clasped each other and she hadn't another comment on that subject.

My legal adviser, a real nobody from nothing, was trying to invent an environment of familial madness from which I could not have hoped to recover. "That is certainly an odd name, in combination with his last name, Charles C. Charley, Mrs. Charley. How did this naming come about?"

"What is your name, sir?" asked my mother politely.

With a boyish grin he replied, "Edward Johnson, ma'am."

"Ha! Ha! Ha!" said my mother.

When it was my turn, he asked, "And weren't you in love with young Miss Graham, that flirtatious young woman, when you lost your head? Weren't you?"

"Generally speaking," I replied, "there's love in physical union. It's referred to in Western literature as an act of love."

"That's true," he said, not cerebrating noticeably. "And you loved Miss Graham, didn't you?" Here he pointed to her where she sat. Her hair had been washed that early morning. She wore a golden Chinese slip of a dress with little slits, probably to flash her tan calves through. Her sweet round rump nestled in the hard pew of the law.

"I suppose I did," I said.

At last the attorney for the prosecuting victim had a chance at me. He had known Cindy since she was an even younger child than she was a child at present, he said, using just those words. He was close to tears. Not a hair was rooted in his head. This is description, not adventitious comment, which I can't afford, since I am unpleasantly hirsute.

Even now, time having awarded some dimension, I don't understand his line of questioning nor the line of questioning of my own brainless lawyer. I had pleaded guilty. I was not opposed to punishment, since our happy performance, it turned out, had a criminal aspect. Still they talked. I realize they had their training to consider—all those years at school. Men like these must milk the moment or sleep forever.

"Well," he began, blinking a tear, "Charles C. Charley, you have told us that you loved that little girl at that moment but did not love her before or after and have not since?"

"I have no reason to lie," I said. "I am in the hand of God."

"Who?" the judge shouted.

Then they all mumbled together in an effort to figure out what could be done with the contemptible use of pious nomenclature. They could not say, of course, that we are not in the hand of God when, for all they knew, we were.

Mr. Graham's gleaming attorney returned to me. "Mr. Charley, did you love Cindy Graham at that moment?"

"I did," I said.

"But you do not love her now?" he asked.

"I haven't thought about it," I said.

"Would you marry her?" he demanded, twisting his head toward the jury. He felt sly.

"She's just a child," I said. "How could I marry her? Marriage requires all sorts of responsibility. She isn't ready for anything like that. And besides, the age difference . . . it's too great. Be realistic," I adjured his muddled head.

"You would *not* marry her?" he asked, his voice rising to a clinch.

"No, sir."

"Good enough to force sex on but not good enough to cherish for life?"

"Well," I said calmly, refusing to respond to his hysteria, and without mentioning names, "actually it's six of one and half a dozen of the other."

"And so you, a mature man, an adult, you took it upon yourself, knowing something about the pitfalls before a young girl, this child, still growing, Cynthia Anne Graham, you took it upon yourself to decide she was ready to have her virginity ravaged to satisfy your own selfish rotten lust."

After that little bit of banter I clammed up. Because Cindy was going to live among them forever, I was so silent that even now I am breathless with self-respect.

These castaways on life's sodden beach were under the impression that I was the first. I was not. I am not an inventive or creative person, I take a cue from the universe, I have never been the first anywhere. Actually, in this case, I was no more than fifth or sixth. I don't say this to be disparaging of Cindy. A person has to start somewhere. Why was Mr. Graham so baffled by truth? Gourmets everywhere begin with voracious appetites before they can come to the finesse of taste. I had seen it happen before; in five or six years, a beautiful and particular woman, she might marry some contributing citizen and resign her light habits to him. None of my adversaries was more than ten years my senior, but their memories were short (as mine would be if I weren't sure at all times to keep in touch with youth).

In the middle of my thinking, while the court waited patiently for a true answer, Cindy burst into wild tears, screaming, "Leave him alone, you leave him alone. It's not his fault if I'm wild. I'll tell the whole world how wild I am if you don't shut up. I made him do it, I made him do it. . . ."

From my narrow-eyed view the court seemed to constrict into a shuddering sailor's knot. Cindy's mother and father unraveled her, and two civil-service employees hustled her out. The opposing lawyers buzzed together and then with the judge. A pair of newspapermen staggered from one convulsive group to another. My mother took advantage of the disorganization to say, "Charles, they're bugheaded."

The paid principals nodded their heads. The judge asked for order, then a recess. My attorney and two cops led me into a brown-paneled room where a board-meeting mahogany table was surrounded by board-meeting chairs. "You didn't give one sensible answer," my attorney complained. "Now listen to me. Just sit down here and keep your mouth shut, for godsakes. I'm going to talk to the Grahams."

Except for some bored surveillance, I was alone for one hour and a half. In that time I reviewed Cindy and all her accessories, also the meaning of truth. I was just tangent to the Great Circle of Life, of which I am one irrevocable diameter, when my mother appeared. She had had time to go shopping for some wheat germ and carrots and apples full of unsprayed bacteria. The state of her health requires these innocent staples. Mr. and Mrs. Graham followed, and my little grimy Cindy. Mrs. Graham kept tissuing some of the black eye stuff off her smeared cheeks. Mr. Graham, sensible when answering or questioning and never devious, said, "All right, Charles, all right. We've decided to withdraw charges. You and Cindy will get married."

"What?" I said.

"You heard me the first time . . . I'm against it. I think a punk like you is better off in jail. For my money, you could rot in jail. I've seen worse guys but not much worse. You took advantage of a damn silly kid. You and Cindy get married next week. Meanwhile you'll be at our house, Charley. Cindy's missed enough school. This is a very important year for her. I'll tell you one thing. You better play it straight, Charley, or I'll split your skull with a kitchen knife."

"Say . . ." I said.

My mother piped up. "Charles," she said, "son, think about it a minute. What'll happen to me if you go to jail? She's very pretty. You're not getting younger. What'll happen to me? Son . . ." she said.

She turned to Mrs. Graham. "It's hard to be old and dependent this way. I hope you have plenty of insurance."

Mrs. Graham patted her shoulder.

My mother regarded this as invitation to enlarge. "When you really think about it, it's all a fuss about nothing. I always say, let them enjoy themselves when they're young. You know," she said, her eyes hazy in the crowded past, "at least it gives you something to look back on."

Mrs. Graham removed her hand and blushed in fear.

"Don't you want to marry me?" asked Cindy, tears starting again.

"Honey . . ." I said.

"Then it's settled," Mr. Graham said. "I'll find a good house in the neighborhood. No children for a while, Charley, she's got to finish school. As for you," he said, getting down to brass tacks, "the truth is, you have a fair business. I want my accountant to go over the books. If they're what I expect, you'll be cooking with gas in six months. You'll be the biggest conditioning outlet in the county. You're a goddamn slob, you haven't begun to realize your potential in a community like ours."

"I wish I could smoke," I said.

"No smoking here," my lawyer said, having brought my entire life to a successful conclusion.

In this way I assuaged the people in charge, and I live with Cindy in events which are current.

Through the agency of my father-in-law I have ac-

quired a first-class food-freezer and refrigerator franchise. If you can imagine anything so reprehensible, it
was obtained right out from under the nose of a man
who has been in the business for thirty years, a man
who dreamt of that franchise as his reward for unceas-
ing labor in the kitchens of America. If someone would
hand me the first stone, I would not be ashamed to throw
it. But at whom?

Living with Cindy has many pleasures. One acquires
important knowledge in the dwelling place of another
generation. First things first, she always has a kind word
for the future. It is my opinion that she will be a marvelous woman in six or seven years. I wish her luck; by
then we will be strangers.

Two Short Sad Stories from a
Long and Happy Life

1. The Used-Boy Raisers

There were two husbands disappointed by eggs.

I don't like them that way either, I said. Make your own eggs. They sighed in unison. One man was livid; one was pallid.

There isn't a drink around here, is there? asked Livid.

Never find one here, said Pallid. Don't look; driest damn house. Pallid pushed the eggs away, pain and disgust his escutcheon.

Livid said, Now really, isn't there a drink? Beer? he hoped.

Nothing, said Pallid, who'd been through the pantries, closets, and refrigerators looking for a white shirt.

You're damn right, I said. I buttoned the high button of my powder-blue duster. I reached under the kitchen table for a brown paper bag full of an embroidery which asked God to Bless Our Home.

I was completing this motto for the protection of my sons, who were also Livid's. It is true that some months earlier, from a far place—the British plains in Africa— he had written hospitably to Pallid: I do think they're fine boys, you understand. I love them too, but Faith is their mother and now Faith is your wife. I'm so much away. If you want to think of them as yours, old man, go ahead.

Why, thank you, Pallid had replied, airmail, overwhelmed. Then he implored the boys, when not in use, to play in their own room. He made all efforts to be kind.

Now as we talked of time past and upon us, I pierced the ranch house that nestles in the shade of a cloud and a Norway maple, just under the golden script.

Ha-ha, said Livid, dripping coffee on his pajama pants, you'll never guess whom I met up with, Faith.

Who? I asked.

Saw your old boy friend Clifford at the Green Coq. He looks well. One thing must be said, he addressed Pallid, she takes good care of her men.

True, said Pallid.

How is he? I asked coolly. What's he doing? I haven't seen him in two years.

Oh, you'll never guess. He's marrying. A darling girl. She was with him. Little tootsies, little round bottom, little tummy—she must be twenty-two, but she looks seventeen. One long yellow braid down her back. A darling girl. Stubby nose, fat little underlip. Her eyes put on in pencil. Shoulders down like a dancer . . . slender neck. Oh, darling, darling.

You certainly observed her, said Pallid.

I have a functioning retina, said Livid. Then he went on. Better watch out, Faith. You'd be surprised, the dear little chicks are hatching out all over the place. All the sunny schoolgirls rolling their big black eyes. I hope you're really settled this time. To me, whatever is under the dam is in another county; however, in my life you remain an important person historically, he said. And that's why I feel justified in warning you. I must warn you. Watch out, sweetheart! he said, leaning forward to whisper harshly and give me a terrible bellyache.

What's all this about? asked Pallid innocently. In the first place, she's settled . . . and then she's still an attractive woman. Look at her.

Oh yes, said Livid, looking. An attractive woman. Magnificent, sometimes.

We were silent for several seconds in honor of that generous remark.

Then Livid said, Yes, magnificent, but I just wanted to warn you, Faith.

He pushed his eggs aside finally and remembered Clifford. A mystery wrapped in an enigma . . . I wonder why he wants to marry.

I don't know, it just ties a man down, I said.

And yet, said Pallid seriously, what would I be without marriage? In luminous recollection—a gay dog, he replied.

At this moment, the boys entered: Richard the horse thief and Tonto the crack shot.

Daddy! they shouted. They touched Livid, tickled him, unbuttoned his pajama top, whistled at the several gray hairs coloring his chest. They tweaked his ear and rubbed his beard the wrong way.

Well, well, he cautioned. How are you boys, have you been well? You look fine. Sturdy. How are your grades? he inquired. He dreamed that they were just up from Eton for the holidays.

I don't go to school, said Tonto. I go to the park.

I'd like to hear the child read, said Livid.

Me. I can read, Daddy, said Richard. I have a book with a hundred pages.

Well, well, said Livid. Get it.

I kindled a fresh pot of coffee. I scrubbed cups and harassed Pallid into opening a sticky jar of damson-plum jam. Very shortly, what could be read, had been, and Livid, knotting the tie strings of his pants vigorously, approached me at the stove. Faith, he admonished, that boy can't read a tinker's damn. Seven years old.

Eight years old, I said.

Yes, said Pallid, who had just remembered the soap cabinet and was rummaging in it for a pint. If they were my sons in actuality as they are in everyday life, I would send them to one of the good parochial schools in the neighborhood where reading is taught. Reading. St. Bartholomew's, St. Bernard's, St. Joseph's.

Livid became deep purple and gasped. Over my dead body. *Merde,* he said in deference to the children. I've said, yes, you may think of the boys as your own, but if I ever hear they've come within an inch of that church, I'll run you through, you bastard. I was fourteen years old when in my own good sense I walked out of that grotto of deception, head up. You sonofabitch, I don't give a damn how *au courant* it is these days, how gracious to be seen under a dome on Sunday. . . . Shit! Hypocrisy. Corruption. Cave dwellers. Idiots. Morons.

Recalling childhood and home, poor Livid writhed in his seat. Pallid listened, head to one side, his brows gathering the onsets of grief.

You know, he said slowly, we iconoclasts . . . we free-thinkers . . . we latter-day masons . . . we idealists . . .

we dreamers . . . we are never far from our nervous old mother, the Church. She is never far from us.

Wherever we are, we can hear, no matter how faint, her hourly bells, tolling the countryside, reverberating in the cities, bringing to our civilized minds the passionate deed of Mary. Every hour on the hour we are startled with remembrance of what was done for us. FOR US.

Livid muttered in great pain, Those bastards, oh oh oh, those contemptible, goddannable bastards. Do we have to do the nineteenth century all over again? All right, he bellowed, facing us all, I'm ready. That Newman! He turned to me for approval.

You know, I said, this subject has never especially interested me. It's your little dish of lava.

Pallid spoke softly, staring past the arched purple windows of his soul. I myself, although I lost God a long time ago, have never lost faith.

What the hell are you talking about, you moron? roared Livid.

I have never lost my love for the wisdom of the Church of the World. When I go to sleep at night, I inadvertently pray. I also do so when I rise. It is not to God, it is to that unifying memory out of childhood. The first words I ever wrote were: What are the sacraments? Faith, can you ever forget your old grandfather intoning Kaddish? It will sound in your ears forever.

Are you kidding? I was furious to be drawn into their conflict. Kaddish? What do I know about Kaddish. Who's dead? You know my opinions perfectly well. I believe in the Diaspora, not only as a fact but a tenet. I'm against Israel on technical grounds. I'm very disappointed that they decided to become a nation in my life-time. I believe in the Diaspora. After all, they *are* the chosen people. Don't laugh. They really are. But once they're huddled in one little corner of a desert, they're like anyone else: Frenchies, Italians, temporal nationalities. Jews have one hope only—to remain a remnant in the basement of world affairs—no, I mean something else—a splinter in the toe of civilizations, a victim to aggravate the conscience.

Livid and Pallid were astonished at my outburst, since I rarely express my opinion on any serious matter but only live out my destiny, which is to be, until my expiration date, laughingly the servant of man.

I continued. I hear they don't even look like Jews any more. A bunch of dirt farmers with no time to read.

They're your own people, Pallid accused, dilating in the nostril, clenching his jaw. And they're under the severest attack. This is not the time to revile them.

I had resumed my embroidery. I sighed. My needle was now deep in the clouds which were pearl gray and late afternoon. I am only trying to say that they aren't meant for geographies but for history. They are not supposed to take up space but to continue in time.

They looked at me with such grief that I decided to consider all sides of the matter. I said, Christ probably had all that trouble—now that you mention it—because he knew he was going to gain the whole world but he forgot Jerusalem.

When you married us, said Pallid, and accused me, didn't you forget Jerusalem?

I never forget a thing, I said. Anyway, guess what. I

just read somewhere that England is bankrupt. The country is wadded with installment paper.

Livid's hand trembled as he offered Pallid a light. Nonsense, he said. That's not true. Nonsense. The great British Island is the tight little fist of the punching arm of the Commonwealth.

What's true is true, I said, smiling.

Well, I said, since no one stirred, do you think you'll ever get to work today? Either of you?

Oh, my dear, I haven't even seen you and the boys in over a year. It's quite pleasant and cozy here this morning, said Livid.

Yes, isn't it? said Pallid, the surprised host. Besides, it's Saturday.

How do you find the boys? I asked Livid, the progenitor.

American, American, rowdy, uncontrolled. But you look well, Faith. Plumper, but womanly and well.

Very well, said Pallid, pleased.

But the boys, Faith. Shouldn't they be started on something? Just lining up little plastic cowboys. It's silly, really.

They're so young, apologized Pallid, the used-boy raiser.

You'd both better go to work, I suggested, knotting the pearl-gray late-afternoon thread. Please put the dishes in the sink first. Please. I'm sorry about the eggs.

Livid yawned, stretched, peeked at the clock, sighed. Saturday or no, alas, my time is not my own. I've got an appointment downtown in about forty-five minutes, he said.

I do too, said Pallid. I'll join you on the subway.

I'm taking a cab, said Livid.

I'll split it with you, said Pallid.

They left for the bathroom, where they shared things nicely—shaving equipment, washstand, shower, and so forth.

I made the beds and put the aluminum cot away. Livid would find a hotel room by nightfall. I did the dishes and organized the greedy day; dinosaurs in the morning, park in the afternoon, peanut butter in between, and at the end of it all, to reward us for a week of beans endured, a noble rib roast with little onions, dumplings, and pink applesauce.

Faith, I'm going now, Livid called from the hall. I put my shopping list aside and went to collect the boys, who were wandering among the rooms looking for Robin Hood. Go say goodbye to your father, I whispered.

Which one? they asked.

The real father, I said. Richard ran to Livid. They shook hands manfully. Pallid embraced Tonto and was kissed eleven times for his affection.

Goodbye now, Faith, said Livid. Call me if you want anything at all. Anything at all, my dear. Warmly with sweet propriety he kissed my cheek. Ascendant, Pallid kissed me with considerable business behind the ear.

Goodbye, I said to them.

I must admit that they were at last clean and neat, rather attractive, shiny men in their thirties, with the grand affairs of the day ahead of them. Dark night, the search for pleasure and oblivion were well ahead. Goodbye, I said, have a nice day. Goodbye, they said once more, and set off in pride on paths which are not my concern.

2. A Subject of Childhood

At home one Saturday and every Saturday, Richard drew eight-by-eleven portraits of stick men waving their arms. Tonto held a plastic horse in his hand and named it Tonto because its eyes were painted blue as his had been. I revised the hem of last year's dress in order to be up to the minute, chic, and *au courant* in the midst of spring. Strangers would murmur, "Look at her, isn't she wonderful? Who's her couturier?"

Clifford scrubbed under the shower, singing a Russian folk song. He rose in a treble of cold water to high C, followed by the scourging of the flesh. At last after four hots and three colds, he was strong and happy and he entered the living room, a steaming emanation. His face was round and rosy. He was noticeably hairless on the head. What prevented rain and shower water from running foolishly down his face? Heavy dark down-sloping brows. Beneath these his eyes were round and dark, amazed. This Clifford, my close friend, was guileless. He would not hurt a fly and he was a vegetarian.

As always, he was glad to see us. He had wrapped a large sun-bathing towel around his damp body. "Behold the man!" he shouted, and let the towel fall. He stood for a moment, gleaming and pleasant. Richard and Tonto glanced at him. "Cover yourself, for God's sakes, Clifford," I said.

"Take it easy, Faith," he called to the ear of reason. "the world is changing." Actually propriety did not embarrass him. It did not serve him. He peeked from behind the rubber plant where his pants, under and over, were heaped. When he reappeared, snapped and buttoned, he said, "Wake up, wake up. What's everyone slouching around for?" He poked Richard in the tummy. "A little muscle tone there, boy. Wake up."

Richard said, "I want to draw, Clifford."

"You can draw any time. I'm not always here. Draw tomorrow, Rich. Come on—fight me, boy. Fight. Come on . . . let's go, get me. You better get started, Richy, 'cause I'm gonna really punch you one. Here I come, ready or not!"

"Here *I* come," said Tonto, dropping his horse, and he whacked Clifford hard across the kidneys.

"Who did that?" asked Clifford. "What boy did that?"

"Me, me," said Tonto, jumping up and down. "Did I hurt you bad?"

"Killed me, yes sir, yes you did, and now I'm going to get *you*." He whirled. "I'm going to tickle you, that's what." He raised Tonto high above his head, a disposable item, then pitched him into the air-foam belly of the couch.

Richard tiptoed with the Teddy bear to a gentle rise, the sofa cushion, from which he crowned Clifford three times.

"Oh, I'm getting killed," cried Clifford. "They're all after me. They're very rough." Richard kicked him in the shin. "That's it," said Clifford. "Get it out! Get it all out! Boys! Out! Out!"

Tonto spit right into his eye. He wiped his cheek. He feinted and dodged the Teddy bear that was coming down again on his bowed head. Tonto leaped onto his back and got hold of his ears. "Ouch," said Clifford.

Richard found a tube of rubber cement in the bookcase and squirted it at Clifford's hairy chest.

"I'm wild," said Richard. "I am, I'm wild."

"So am I," said Tonto. "I'm the wildest boy in the whole park." He tugged at Clifford's ears. "I'll ride you away. I'm an elephant boy."

"He's a lazy camel," screamed Richard. "Bubbles, I want you to work."

"Pretend I'm the djinn," said Tonto in a high wail. "Giddap, Clifford."

"Me, me, me," said Richard, sinking to the floor. "It's me. I'm a poison snake," he said, slithering to Clifford's foot. "I'm a poison snake," he said, resting his chin on Clifford's instep. "I'm a terrible poison snake," he swore. Then he raised his head like the adder he is, and after a prolonged hiss, with all his new front teeth, he bit poor Clifford above the bone, in his Achilles' heel, which is his weak left ankle.

"Oh no, oh no . . ." Clifford moaned, then folded neatly at all joints.

"Mommy, Mommy, Mommy," cried Richard, for Clifford fell, twelve stone, on him.

"Oh, it's me," screamed Tonto, an elephant boy thrown by his horse, headlong into a trap of table legs.

And he was the one I reached first. I hugged him to my lap. "Mommy," he sobbed, "my head hurts me. I wish

I could get inside you." Richard lay, a crushed snake in the middle of the floor, without breath, without tears, angry.

Well, what of Clifford? He had hoisted his sorrowful self into an armchair and lay there lisping on a bloody tongue which he himself had bitten, "Faith, Faith, the accumulator, the accumulator!"

Bruised and tear-stricken, the children agreed to go to bed. They forgot to say it was too early to nap. They forgot to ask for their bears. They lay side by side and clutched each other's thumb. Here was the love that myth or legend has imposed on brothers.

I re-entered the living room where Clifford sat, a cone like an astrologer's hat on his skin-punctured place. Just exactly there, universal energies converged. The stationary sun, the breathless air in which the planets swing were empowered now to make him well, to act, in their remarkable art, like aspirin.

"We've got to have a serious talk," he said. "I really can't take those kids. I mean, Faith, you know yourself I've tried and tried. But you've done something to them, corrupted their instincts in some way or other. Here we were, having an absolutely marvelous time, rolling around making all kinds of free noise, and look what happened—like every other time, someone got hurt. I mean I'm really hurt. We should have all been relaxed. Easy. It should have been all easy. Our bodies should have been so easy. No one should've been hurt, Faith."

"Do you mean it's my fault you all got hurt?"

"No doubt about it, Faith, you've done a rotten job."

"Rotten job?" I said.

"Lousy," he said.

I gave him one more chance. "Lousy?" I asked.

"Oh my god! Stinking!" he said.

Therefore, the following—a compendium of motivations and griefs, life to date:

Truthfully, Mondays through Fridays—because of success at work—my ego is hot; I am a star; whoever can be warmed by me, I may oblige. The flat scale stones of abuse that fly into that speedy atmosphere are utterly consumed. Untouched, I glow my little thermodynamic way.

On Saturday mornings in my own home, however, I face the sociological law called the Obtrusion of Incontrovertibles. For I have raised these kids, with one hand typing behind my back to earn a living. I have raised them all alone without a father to identify themselves with in the bathroom like all the other little boys in the playground. Laugh. I was forced by inclement management into a yellow-dog contract with Bohemia, such as it survives. I have stuck by it despite the encroachments of kind relatives who offer ski pants, piano lessons, tickets to the rodeo. Meanwhile I have serviced Richard and Tonto, taught them to keep clean and hold an open heart on the subjects of childhood. We have in fact risen mightily from toilets in the hall and scavenging in great cardboard boxes at the Salvation Army for underwear and socks. It has been my perversity to do this alone, except for the one year their father was living in Chicago with Claudia Lowenstill and she was horrified that he only sent bicycles on the fifth birthday. A whole year of gas and electricity, rent and phone payments followed. One day she caught him in the swiveling light of truth, a grand figure who took a strong stand on a barrel of soapsuds and went down clean. He is now on the gold coast of another continent, enchanted by the survival of clandestine civilizations. Courts of kitchen drama cannot touch him.

All the same, I gave Clifford one more opportunity to renege and be my friend. I said, "Stinking? I raised them lousy?"

This time he didn't bother to answer because he had become busy gathering his clothes from different parts of the room.

Air was filtering out of my two collapsing lungs. Water rose, bubbling to enter, and I would have died of instantaneous pneumonia—something I never have heard of—if my hand had not got hold of a glass ash tray and, entirely apart from my personal decision, flung it.

Clifford was on his hands and knees looking for the socks he'd left under the armchair on Friday. His back was to me; his head convenient to the trajectory. And he would have passed away a blithering idiot had I not been blind with tears and only torn off what is anyway a vestigial ear lobe.

Still, Clifford is a gentle person, a consortment of sweet dispositions. The sight of all the blood paralyzed him. He hulked, shuddering; he waited on his knees to be signaled once more by Death, the Sheriff from the Styx.

"You don't say things like that to a woman," I whispered. "You damn stupid jackass. You just don't say anything like that to a woman. Wash yourself, moron, you're bleeding to death."

I left him alone to tie a tourniquet around his windpipe or doctor himself according to present-day plans for administering first aid in the Great Globular and Coming War.

I tiptoed into the bedroom to look at the children. They were asleep. I covered them and kissed Tonto, my baby, and "Richard, what a big boy you are," I said. I kissed him too. I sat on the floor, rubbing my cheek on Richard's rubbly fleece blanket until their sweet breathing in deep sleep quieted me.

A couple of hours later Richard and Tonto woke up picking their noses, sneezing, grumpy, then glad. They admired the ticktacktoes of Band-Aid I had created to honor their wounds. Richard ate soup and Tonto ate ham. They didn't inquire about Clifford, since he had a key which had always opened the door in or out.

That key lay at rest in the earth of my rubber plant. I felt discontinued. There was no one I wanted to offer it to.

"Still hungry, boys?" I asked. "No, sir," said Tonto. "I'm full up to here," leveling at the eyes.

"I'll tell you what," I came through with a stunning notion. "Go on down and play."

"Don't shove, miss," said Richard.

I looked out the front window. Four flights below, armed to the teeth, Lester Stukopf waited for the enemy. Carelessly I gave Richard this classified information. "Is he all alone?" asked Richard.

"He is," I said.

"O.K., O.K." Richard gazed sadly at me. "Only, Faith, remember, I'm going down because I feel like it. Not because you told me."

"Well, naturally," I said.

"Not me," said Tonto.

"Oh, don't be silly, you go too, Tonto. It's so nice and sunny. Take your new guns that Daddy sent you. Go on, Tonto."

"No, sir, I hate Richard and I hate Lester. I hate those guns. They're baby guns. He thinks I'm a baby. You better send him a picture."

"Oh, Tonto——"

"He thinks I suck my thumb. He thinks I wet my bed. That's why he sends me baby guns."

"No, no, honey. You're no baby. Everybody knows you're a big boy."

"He is not," said Richard. "And he does so suck his thumb and he does so wet his bed."

"Richard," I said, "Richard, if you don't have anything good to say, shut your rotten mouth. That doesn't help Tonto, to keep reminding him."

"Goodbye," said Richard, refusing to discuss, but very high and first-born. Sometimes he is nasty, but he is never lazy. He returned in forty-five seconds from the first floor to shout, "As long as he doesn't wet my bed, what do I care?"

Tonto did not hear him. He was brushing his teeth, which he sometimes does vigorously seven times a day, hoping they will loosen. I think they are loosening.

I served myself hot coffee in the living room. I organized comfort in the armchair, poured the coffee black into a white mug that said MAMA, tapped cigarette ash into a ceramic hand-hollowed by Richard. I looked into the square bright window of daylight to ask myself the sapping question: What is man that woman lies down to adore him?

At the very question mark Tonto came softly, sneaky in socks, to say, "I have to holler something to Richard, Mother."

"Don't lean out that window, Tonto. Please, it makes me nervous."

"I have to tell him something."

"No."

"Oh yes," he said. "It's awful important, Faith. I really *have* to."

How could I permit it? If he should fall, everyone would think I had neglected them, drinking beer in the kitchen or putting eye cream on at the vanity table behind closed doors. Besides, I would be bereaved forever. My grandmother mourned all her days for some kid who'd died of earache at the age of five. All the other children, in their own municipal-pension and federal-welfare years, gathered to complain at her deathside when she was ninety-one and heard her murmur, "Oh, oh, Anita, breathe a little, try to breathe, my little baby."

With tears in my eyes I said, "O.K., Tonto, I'll hold onto you. You can tell Richard anything you have to."

He leaned out onto the air. I held fast to one thick little knee. "Richie," he howled. "Richie, hey, Richie!" Richard looked up, probably shielding his eyes, searching for the voice. "Richie, hey, listen, I'm playing with your new birthday-present army fort and all them men."

Then he banged the window shut as though he knew nothing about the nature of glass and tore into the bathroom to brush his teeth once more in triumphant ritual.

Singing through toothpaste and gargle, "I bet he's mad," and in lower key, "He deserves it, he stinks."

"So do you," I shouted furiously. While I sighed for my grandmother's loss, he had raised up his big mouth against his brother. "You really stink!"

"Now listen to me. I want you to get out of here. Go on down and play. I need ten minutes all alone. Anthony, I might kill you if you stay up here."

He reappeared, smelling like peppermint sticks at Christmas. He stood on one foot, looked up into my high eyes, and said, "O.K., Faith. Kill me."

I had to sit immediately then, so he could believe I was his size and stop picking on me.

"Please," I said gently, "go out with your brother. I have to think, Tonto."

"I don't wanna. I don't have to go anyplace I don't wanna," he said. "I want to stay right here with you."

"Oh, please, Tonto, I have to clean the house. You won't be able to do a thing or start a good game or anything."

"I don't care," he said. "I want to stay here with you. I want to stay right next to you."

"O.K., Tonto. O.K. I'll tell you what, go to your room for a couple of minutes, honey, go ahead."

"No," he said, climbing onto my lap. "I want to be a baby and stay right next to you every minute."

"Oh, Tonto," I said, "please, Tonto." I tried to pry him loose, but he put his arm around my neck and curled up right there in my lap, thumb in mouth, to be my baby.

"Oh, Tonto," I said, despairing of one solitary minute. "Why can't you go play with Richard? You'll have fun."

"No," he said, "I don't care if Richard goes away, or Clifford. They can go do whatever they wanna do. I don't even care. I'm never gonna go away. I'm gonna stay right next to you forever, Faith."

"Oh, Tonto," I said. He took his thumb out of his mouth and placed his open hand, its fingers stretching wide, across my breast. "I love you, Mama," he said.

"Love," I said. "Oh love, Anthony, I know."

I held him so and rocked him. I cradled him. I closed my eyes and leaned on his dark head. But the sun in its course emerged from among the water towers of downtown office buildings and suddenly shone white and bright on me. Then through the short fat fingers of my son, interred forever, like a black and white barred king in Alcatraz, my heart lit up in stripes.

In Time Which Made a Monkey
of Us All

No doubt that is Eddie Teitelbaum on the topmost step of 1434, a dark-jawed, bossy youth in need of repair. He is dredging a cavity with a Fudgsicle stick. He is twitching the cotton in his ear. He is sniffing and snarling and swallowing spit because of rotten drainage. But he does not give a damn. Physicalities aside, he is only knee-deep so far in man's inhumanity; he is reconciled to his father's hair-shirted Jacob, Itzik Halbfunt; he is resigned to his place in this brick-lined Utrillo which runs east and west, flat in the sun, a couple of thousand stoop steps. On each step there is probably someone he knows. For the present, no names.

Now look at the little kids that came in those days to buzz at his feet. That is what they did, they gathered in this canyon pass, rumbling at the knee of his glowering personality. Some days he heeded them a long and wiggily line which they followed up and down the street, around the corner, and back to 1434.

On dark days he made elephants, dogs, rabbits, and long-tailed mice for them out of pipe cleaners. "You can also make a neat ass cleaner this way," he told them for a laugh, which turned their mothers entirely against him. Well, he was a poor sloppy bastard then, worked Saturdays, Sundays, summers, and holidays, no union contract in his father's pet shop. But penny-wise as regards the kids, he was bubble-gum foolish, for bubble gum strengthens the jaw. He never worried about teeth but approved of dentures and, for that matter, all prostheses.

In the end, man will probably peel his skin (said Eddie) to favor durable plastics, at which time, kaput the race problem. A man will be any color he chooses or translucent too, if the shape and hue of intestines can be made fashionable. Eddie had lots of advance information which did not turn a hair of his head, for he talked of the ineluctable future; but all his buddies, square or queer, clever and sentimental, pricked their ears in tears.

He also warned them of the spies who peeked from windows or plopped like stones on the street which was the kids' by all unentailed rights. Mrs. Goredinsky, head spy the consistency of fresh putty, sat on an orange crate every morning, her eye on the door of 1434. Also Mrs. Green, Republican poll watcher in November—the rest of the year she waited in her off-the-street doorway, her hand trembling, her head turning one way, then the other.

"Tennis, anyone?" asked Carl Clop, the super's son.

"Let her live," said Eddie, marking time.

Then one day old Clop, the super, rose from the cellar, scrambling the kids before him with the clatter of bottle tops. He took a stance five steps below Eddie, leaned on his broom, and prepared to make conversation.

"What's the matter, son?" he asked. "Where's your pals?"

"Under the kitchen table," said Eddie. "They got juiced on apricot nectar."

"Go on, Eddie; you got an in. Who's the bum leaves Kleenex in the halls?"

"I don't know. Goredinsky has a cold for months."

"Aah, her, what you got against her, a old pot of cabbage soup? You always make a remark on her."

Out of a dark window in second-floor front a tiny voice sang to the tune of "My Country, 'tis of Thee":

"Mrs. Goredinsky was a spy
Caught by the FBI.
Tomorrow she will die—
Won't that be good?"

"Get a load of that, Clop," said Eddie. "Nobody has any privacy around here, you notice? Listen to me, Clop, in the country in superbia, every sonofabitch has a garage to tinker in. On account of that, great ideas, brilliant inventions come from out of town. Why the hell shouldn't we produce as fine minds as anybody else?"

Now Eddie was just helping Clop out, talkwise, maintaining relations with authority, so to speak. He would have ended the conversation right then and there, since at that moment he was in the mental act of inventing a cockroach segregator, a device which would kill only that cockroach which emigrated out of its pitchy crack into the corn flakes of people. If properly conceived and delicately contrived, all the other cockroaches would be left alone to gum up the lathes and multiply and finally inherit the entire congressional district. Why not?

"Not so dumb," said Mr. Clop. "Privacy." Then he let

Eddie have a bewhiskered, dead-eye, sideways leer. "What you need privacy for, you? To stick it into girls?"

No reply.

Clop retrieved the conversation. "So that's how it goes, that's how they get ahead of us, the farmers. What do you know? How come someone don't figure it out, to educate you kids up a little, especially in summer? The city's the one pays the most taxes. Anyway, what the hell you do on the stoop all day? How come Carl hangs out in front of Michailovitch, morning noon night, every time I look up? Come on, get the hell off the stoop here, you Teitelbaum," he yelled. "Stupids. Stick the Kleenex in your pocket." He gave Eddie a splintery whisk with the broom. He turned away, frowning, thinking. "Go 'way, bums," he mumbled at two loitering infants, maybe four years old.

Nevertheless, Clop was a man of grave instinct, a serious man. Three days later he offered Eddie the key to the bicycle and carriage room of 1436, the corner and strategic building.

"For thinking up inventions," said Clop. "What are we, animals?" He went on to tell that he was proud to be associated with scientific research. So many boys were out bumming, on the tramp, tramp, tramp. Carl, his own son, looked bad, played poker day and night under the stairs with Shmul, the rabbi's son, a Yankee in a skullcap.° Therefore, Clop begged Eddie to persuade Carl to do a little something in his line of thinking and follow-through. He really liked science very much,

° *Yankee in a Skullcap: My Day & Night in the East Bronx,* Shmul Klein, Mitzvah Press

Mr. Clop said, but needed a little encouragement, since he had no mother.

"O.K., O.K." Eddie was willing. "He can help me figure out a rocket to the moon."

"The moon?" Mr. Clop asked. He peeked out the cellar window at a piece of noonday sky.

Right before Eddie's mirage-making eyes for his immediate use was a sink, electricity, gas outlets, and assorted plumbing pipes. What else is basic to any laboratory? Do you think that the Institute for Advanced Studies started out any stronger than that, or all the little padlocked cyclotron houses? The beginning of everything is damp and small, but wide-armed oaks— according to myth, legend, and the folk tales of the people—from solitary acorns grow.

Eddie's first chore was the perfection of the cockroach segregator. At cost plus 6 per cent, he trailed some low-voltage wire all around local kitchen baseboards, which immediately returned to its gummy environment under the linoleum the cockroach which could take a hint. It electrocuted the stubborn fools not meant by Darwin anyway to survive.

There was nothing particularly original in this work. Eddie would be the first to concede that he had been thinking about the country and cows all summer, as well as barbed wire, and had simply applied recollected knowledge to the peculiar conditions of his environment.

"What a hell of a summer this is turning into," said Carl, plucking a bug off the lab's wire. "I mean, we ought to have some fun too, Eddie. How about it? I mean, if we were a club, we would be more well rounded."

"Everyone wants fun," said Eddie.

"I don't mean real fun," said Carl. "We could be a science club. But just you and me—— No, I'm sick of that crap. Get some more guys in. Make it an organization, Eddie."

"Why not?" said Eddie, anxious to get to work.

"Great. I've been thinking of some names. How's . . . Advanseers . . . Get it?"

"Stinks."

"I thought of a funny one . . . like on those little cards. How about The Thimkers?"

"Very funny."

Carl didn't press it. "All right. But we have to get some more members."

"Two," said Eddie, thinking a short laugh.

"Well, O.K. But, Eddie, what about girls? I mean, after all, women have the vote a long time. They're doctors and . . . What about Madame Curie? There's others."

"Please, Carl, lay off. We got about thirteen miles of wire left. I got to figure out something."

Carl couldn't stop. He liked girls all around him, he said. They made him a sunny, cheerful guy. He could think of wonderful witticisms when they were present. Especially Rita Niskov and Stella Rosenzweig.

He would like to go on, describing, as an example, the Spitz twins, how they were so top-heavy but with hips like boys. Hadn't Eddie seen them afloat at the Seymour Street Pool, water-winged by their airtight tits?

Also darling little Stella Rosenzweig, like a Vassar girl despite being only in third-term high. When you danced with her, you could feel something like pinpricks, be-

154

cause although she was little she was extremely pointed.

Eddie was absolutely flipped by a ground swell of lust just before lunch. To save himself, he coldly said, "No, no. No girls. Saturday nights they can come over for a little dancing, a little petting. Fix up the place. No girls in the middle of the week."

He promised, however, to maintain an open line between Carl and the Spitz twins by recruiting for immediate membership their brother Arnold. That was a lucky, quiet choice. Arnold needed a corner in which to paint. He stated that daylight would eventually disappear and with it the myths about northlight. He founded in that dark cellar a school of painters called the Light Breakers, who still work together in a loft on East Twenty-ninth Street under two 25-watt bulbs.

On Carl's recommendation Shmul Klein was ingathered, a great fourth hand, but Eddie said no card tables. Shmul had the face of an unentrammeled guy. Did he make book after school? No, no, he said, rumors multiplied: the truth was single.

He was a journalist of life, as Eddie was a journeyman in knowledge. When questioned about his future, he would guess that he was destined to trip over grants, carrying a fearsome load of scholarships on his way to a soft job in advertising, using a fraction of his potential.

Well, there were others, of course, who glinted around, seeking membership under the impression that a neighborhood cat house was being established. Eddie laughed and pointed to a market glutted by individual initiative, not to mention the way the bottom has fallen out of the virgin as moral counterweight.

It took time out of Eddie to be a club. Whole afternoons and weekends were lost for public reasons. The boys asked him to hold open meetings so that the club's actual disposition would be appreciated by the parents of girls. Eddie talked then on "The Dispersal of the Galaxies and the Conservation of Matter." Carl applauded twice, in an anarchy of enthusiasm. Mr. Clop listened, was impressed, asked what he could do for them, and then tied their wattage into Mrs. Goredinsky's meter.

Eddie offered political lectures, too, as these are times which, if man were human, could titillate his soul. From the four-by-six room which Eddie shared with Itzik Halbfunt, his father's monkey, he saw configurations of disaster revise the sky before anyone even smelled smoke.

"Who was the enemy?" he asked, to needle a little historicity into his clubmates. "Was it the People of the Sea? Troy? Rome? The Saracens? The Huns? The Russians? The colonies in Africa, the stinking proletariat? The hot owners of capital?"

Typically he did not answer. He let them weave these broad questions on poor pinheaded looms while he slipped into Michailovitch's for a celery tonic.

He shared his profits from the cockroach segregator with the others. This way they took an interest and were courteous enough to heed his philosophic approach, as did the clients to whom he pointed out a human duty to interfere with nature as little as possible except for food-getting (survival), a seminal tragedy which obtains in the wild forests as well.

Reading, thinking on matters beyond the scope of the physical and chemical sciences carried his work from

the idealistic cockroach segregator to a telephone dial
system for people on relief within a ten-block radius
—and finally to the well-known War Attenuator, which
activated all his novitiate lab assistants but featured his
own lonely patience.

"Eddie, Eddie, you take too much time," said his
father. "What about us?"

"You," said Eddie.

How could he forget his responsibilities at the Teitelbaum Zoo, a pet shop where three or four mutts, scabby
with sawdust, slept in the window? A hundred gallons
of goldfish were glassed inside, four canaries singing tu-
wit-tu-wu—all waited for him to dump the seeds, the
hash, the mash into their dinner buckets. Poor Itzik
Halbfunt, the monkey from Paris, France, waited too,
nibbling his beret. Itzik looked like Mr. Teitelbaum's
uncle who had died of Jewishness in the epidemics of
'40, '41. For this reason he would never be sold. "Too
bad," is an outsider's comment, as a certain local Italian
would have paid maybe $45 for that monkey.

In sorrow Mr. Teitelbaum had turned away forever
from his neighbor, man, and for life, then, he squinted
like a cat and hopped like a bird and drooped like a dog.
Like a parrot, all he could say and repeat when Eddie
made his evening break was, "Eddie, don't leave the
door open, me and the birds will fly away."

"If you got wings, Papa, fly," said Eddie. And that was
Eddie's life for years and years, from childhood on: he
shoveled dog shit and birdseed, watching the goldfish
float and feed and die in a big glass of water far away
from China.

One Monday morning in July, bright and hot and

early, Eddie called the boys together for assignments in reconnaissance and mapping. Carl knew the basement extremely well, but Eddie wanted a special listing of doors and windows, their conditions established. There were three buildings involved in this series, 1432, 1434, 1436. He requested that they keep a diary in order to arrive at viable statistics on how many ladies used the laundry facilities at what hours, how hot the hot water generally was at certain specific times.

"Because we are going to work with gases now. Gas expands, compresses, diffuses, and may be liquefied. If there is any danger involved at any point, I will handle it and be responsible. Just don't act like damn fools. I promise you," he added bitterly, "a lot of fun."

He asked them to develop a little competence with tools. Carl as the son of Clop, plumber, electrician, and repairman, was a happy, aggressive teacher. In the noisy washing-machine hours of morning, under Carl's supervision, they drilled barely visible holes in the basement walls and pipe-fitted long-wear rubber tubes. The first series of tests required a network of delicate ducts.

"I am the vena cava and the aorta," Eddie paraphrased. "Whatever goes from me must return to me. You be the engineers. Figure out the best way to nourish all outlying areas."

By "nourish," Shmul pointed out, he really meant "suffocate."

On the twenty-ninth of July they were ready. At 8:13 A.M. the first small-scale, small-area test took place. At 8:12 A.M., just before the moment of pff,° all the business of the cellars was being transacted—garbage transferred

° *The Moment of Pff: An Urban Boyhood*, Shmul Klein, Mitzvah Press

from small cans into large ones; early wide-awake grand-
mas, rocky with insomnia, dumped wash into the big
tubs; boys in swimming trunks rolled baby carriages out
into the cool morning. A coal truck arrived, shifted,
backed up across the sidewalk, stopped, shoved its black
ramp into one sooty cellar window, and commenced to
roar.

Mr. Clop's radio was loud. As he worked, rolling the
cans, hoisting them with Carl's help up the wooden cellar steps, arguing with the coalmen about the right of
way, he listened to the news. He wanted to know if the
sun would roll out, flashy as ever; if there was a chance
for rain, as his brother grew tomatoes in Jersey.

At 8:13 A.M. the alarm clock in the laboratory gave
the ringing word. Eddie touched a button in the sub-
structure of an ordinary glass coffeepot, from whose
spout two tubes proceeded into the wall. A soft hiss followed: the coffeepot steamed and clouded and cleared.

Forty seconds later Mr. Clop howled, "Jesus, who
farted?" although the smell was not quite like that at
all, Eddie the concoctor knew. It was at least *meant* to
be greener, skunkier, closer to the deterrents built into
animals and flowers, but stronger. He was informed immediately of a certain success by the bellows of the coal
delivery men, the high cries of the old ladies.

Satisfied, Eddie touched another button, this at the
base of Mrs. Spitz's reconstructed vacuum cleaner. The
reverse process used no more than two minutes. The
glass clouded, the spout was stoppered, the genie returned.

Eddie knew it would take the boys a little longer to
get free of their observation posts and the people who

were observing them. During that speck of time his heart sank as hearts may do after a great act of love. He suffered a migraine from acceding desolation. When Carl brought excited news, he listened sadly, for what is life? he thought.

"God, great!" cried Carl. "History-making! Crazee! Eddie, Eddie, a mystery! No one knows how what where . . ."

"Yet," Eddie said. "You better quiet down, Carl."

"But listen, Eddie, nobody can figure it out," said Carl. "How long did it last? It ended before that fat dope, Goredinsky, got out of our toilet. She was hollering and pulling up her bloomers and pulling down her dress. I watched from the door. It laid me sidewise. She's not even supposed to use that toilet. It's ours."

"Yeh," said Eddie.

"Wait a minute, wait a minute, listen. My father kept saying, 'Jesus dear, did I forget to open an exhaust someplace? Jesus dear, what did I do? Did I wreck up the flues? Tell me, tell me, give me a hint!' "

"Your father's a very nice old guy," Eddie said coldly.

"Oh, I know that," said Carl.

"Wonderful head," said Arnold, who had just entered.

"Look at my father," Eddie said, taking the dim and agitated view. "Look at him, he sits in that store, he doesn't shave, maybe twice a week. Sometimes he doesn't move an hour or two. His nose drips, so the birds know he's living. That lousy sonofabitch, he used to be a whole expert on world history, he supports a stinking zoo and that filthy monkey that can't even piss straight."
. . . Bitterness for his cramped style and secondhand

pants took his breath away. So he laughed and let them
have the facts. "You know, my old man was so hard up
just before he got married and he got such terrific respect for women (he respects women, let me tell you)
that you know what he did? He snuck into the Bronx
Zoo and he rammed it up a chimpanzee there. You're
surprised, aren't you! Listen to me, they shipped that
baby away to France. If my father'd've owned up,
we'd've been rich. It makes me sore to think about.
He'd've been the greatest buggerer in recorded history.
He'd be wanted in pigsties and stud farms. They'd tele-
graph him a note from Irkutsk to get in on those crazy
cross-pollination experiments. What he could do to winter wheat! That cocksucker tells everyone he went over
to Paris to see if his cousins were alive. He went over to
get my big brother Itzik. To bring him home. To aggravate my mother and me."

"Aw . . ." said Carl.

"So that's it," said Shmul, a late reporter, playing
alongside Eddie. "That's how you got so smart. Constant
competition with an oddball sibling . . . Aha . . ."

"Please," said Arnold, his sketch pad wobbly on his
knee. "Please, Eddie, raise your arms like that again,
like you just did when you were mad. It gives me an
idea."

"Jerks," said Eddie, and spat on the spotless laboratory floor. "A bunch of jerks."

Still and all, the nineteenth-century idea that progress
is immanent is absolutely correct. For his sadness dwin-
dled and early August was a time of hard work and
glorious conviviality. The mystery of the powerful non-
toxic gas from an unknowable source remained. The

boys kept their secret. Outsiders wondered. They knew. They swilled Coke like a regiment which has captured all the enemy pinball machines without registering a single tilt.

Saturday nights at the lab were happy, ringing with 45 r.p.m.'s, surrounded by wonderful women. All kinds of whistling adventures were recorded by Shmul. . . . He had it all written down: how one night Mr. Clop wandered in looking for fuses and found Arnold doing life sketches of Rita Niskov. She held a retort over one breast in order to make technical complications for Arnold, who was ambitious. "Keep it up, keep it up, son," mumbled Clop, to whom it was all a misunderstanding.

And another night Blanchie Spitz took off everything but her drawers and her brassière and because of a teaspoon of rum in a quart and a half of Coke decided to do setting-up exercises to the tune of the "Nutcracker Suite." "Ah, Blanchie," said Carl, nearly nauseous with love, "do me a belly dance, baby." "I don't know what a belly dance is, Carl," she said, and to the count of eight went into a deep knee bend. Arnold lassoed her with Rita's skirt, which he happened to have in his hand. He dragged Blanchie off to a corner, where he slapped her, dressed her, asked her what her fee was and did it include relatives, and before she could answer he slapped her again, then took her home, Rita's skirt flung over one shoulder. This kind of event will turn an entire neighborhood against the most intense chronology of good works. Rita's skirt, hung by a buttonhole, fluttered for two days from the iron cellar railing and was unclaimed. Girls, Shmul editorialized in his little book, live a stone-age life in a blown-glass cave.

Eddie had to receive most of this chattery matter from Shmul. The truth is that Eddie did not take frequent part in the festivities, as Saturday was his father's movie night. Mr. Teitelbaum would have closed the shop, but the manager of the Loew's refused to sell Itzik a ticket. "Show me," said Mr. Teitelbaum, "where it says no monkeys." "Please," said the manager, "this is my busy night." Itzik had never been alone, for although he was a brilliant monkey, in the world of men he is dumb. "Ach," said Mr. Teitelbaum, "you know what it's like to have a monkey for a pet? It's like raising up a moron. You get very attached, no matter what, and very tied down."

"Still and all, things are picking up around here," said Carl.

About a week after the unpleasant incident with the girls (which eventually drove the entire Niskov family about six blocks uptown where they were unknown), Eddie asked for an off-schedule meeting. School was due to begin in three weeks, and he was determined to complete the series which would prove his War Attenuator marketable among the nations.

"Don't exaggerate," said Shmul. "What we have here is a big smell."

"Non-toxic," Eddie pointed out. "No matter how concentrated, non-toxic. Don't forget that, Klein, because that's the beauty of it. An instrument of war that will not kill. Imagine that."

"O.K.," he said. "I concede. So?"

"Shmul, you got an eye. What did the people do during the last test? Did they choke? Did their eyes run? What happened?"

"I already told you, Eddie. Nothing happened. They only ran. They ran like hell. They held their noses and they tore out the door and a couple of kids crawled up the coal ramp. Everybody gave a yelp and then ran."

"What about your father, Carl?"

"Oh, for Christ's sake, if I told you once, I told you twenty times, he got out fast. Then he stood on the steps, holding his nose and figuring who to pass the buck to."

"Well, that's what I mean, boys. It's the lesson of the cockroach segregator. The peaceful guy who listens to the warning of his senses will survive generations of defeat. Who needs the inheritance of the louse with all that miserable virulence in his nucleic acid? Who? I haven't worked out the political strategy altogether, but our job here, anyway, is just to figure out the technology."

"O.K., now the rubber tubes have to be extended up to the first and second floor of 1432, 1434, 1436—the three attached buildings. Do not drill into Michailovitch on the corner, as this could seep into the ice cream containers and fudge and stuff, and I haven't tested out all comestibles. If you work today and tomorrow, we should be done by Thursday. On Friday the test goes forward; by noon we ought have all reports and know what we have. Any questions? Carl, get the tools, you're in charge. I have to fix this goddamn percolator and see what the motor's like. We'll meet on Friday morning. Same time—7:30 A.M."

Then Eddie hurried back to the shop to clean the bird cages which he had forgotten about for days because of the excitement in his mind. Itzik offered him a banana. He accepted. Itzik peeled it for him, then got a banana for himself. He threw the peels into the trash can, for which Eddie kissed him on his foolish face. He jumped to Eddie's shoulder to tease the birds. Eddie did not like him to do this, for those birds will give you psittacosis (said Eddie) if you aggravate them too much. This is an untested hypothesis, but it makes sense; as you know, people who loathe you will sneeze in your face when their mucous membranes are most swollen or when their throat is host to all kinds of cocci.

"Don't, Itzikel," he said gently, and put the monkey down. Then Itzik hung from Eddie's shoulder by one long arm, eating the banana behind his back. "That's how I like to see you," said Mr. Teitelbaum when he looked into the shop. "Once in a while anyway."

Eddie was near the end of a long summer's labor. He could bear being peaceful and happy.

On Friday morning Carl, Arnold, and Shmul waited outside. They had plenty of bubble gum and lollipops in which Eddie had personally invested. They were responsible for maintaining equilibrium among the little children who might panic. They also had notebooks, and in these reports each boy was expected to cover only one building.

Inside, Eddie played a staccato note on the button under the percolator. After that it was very simple. People poured from the three buildings. Tenants on the upper floors, which were not involved, poked their heads out the windows because of the commotion. The controls were so fine that they had gotten only the barest whiff and had assumed it to be the normal smell of morning rising from the cracked back of the fish market three blocks east.

Eddie had agreed not to leave the laboratory until

reports came in from the other boys. He was perplexed when half an hour had passed and they did not appear. There wasn't even a book to read. So he busied himself disconnecting his home-constructed appliances, funneling the residue powder into a paper envelope which he kept in his back pocket. Suddenly he worried about everyone. What could happen to Itsy Bitsy Michailovitch, who sat outside his father's store spinning a yo-yo and singing a no-song to himself all day? He was in fact a goddamn helpless idiot. What about Mrs. Spitz, who would surely stop to put her corset on and would faint away and maybe crack her skull on a piece of rococo mahogany? What about heart failure in people over forty? What about the little Susskind kids? They were so wild, so baffled out of sense, they might jump into the dumb-waiter shaft.

He was scrubbing the sink, trying to uproot his miserable notions, when the door opened. Two policemen came in and put their hands on him. Eddie looked up and saw his father. Their eyes met and because of irrevocable pain, held. That was the moment (said Shmul, later on after that and other facts) that Eddie fell headfirst into the black heart of a deep depression. This despair required all his personal attention for years.

No one could make proper contact with him again, to tell him the news. Did he know that he had caused the death of all his father's stock? Even the three turtles, damn it, every last minnow, even the worms that were the fishes' Sunday dinner had wriggled their last. The birds were dead at the bottom of their clean cages.

Itzik Halbfunt lay in a coma from which he would not recover. He lay in Eddie's bed on Eddie's new mattress, between Eddie's sheets. "Let him die at home," said Mr. Teitelbaum, "not with a bunch of poodles at Speyer's."

He caressed his scrawny shoulder that was itchy and furry and cried, "Halbfunt, Halbfunt, you were my little friend."

No matter how lovingly a person or a doctor rapped at the door to Eddie's mind, Eddie refused to say "come in." Carl Clop called loudly, taking a long distance, local stop, suburban train several times to tell Eddie that it was really he who had thought it would be wonderful to see old Teitelbaum run screaming with hysterical Itzik. For the pleasure this sight would give, Carl had connected the rubber tubes to a small vent between the basement of 1436 and the rear of the pet shop. He had waited at the corner and, sure enough, they had come at last, Mr. Teitelbaum running and Itzik gasping for breath. Clop's bad luck, said Clop, to have a son who wasn't serious.

Eddie was remanded to the custody of Dr. Scott Tully, director of A Home For Boys, in something less than three weeks. The police impounded Shmul's notebooks but learned only literary things about faces and the sex habits of adolescent boys. Also found was an outline of a paper Eddie had planned for the antivivisectionist press, describing his adventures as a self-prepared subject for the gas tolerance experiments. It was entitled NO GUINEA PIG FRONTS FOR ME. As any outsider can judge, this is an insane idea.

Eddie was cared for at A Home For Boys by a white-frocked attendant, cross-eyed and muscle-bound, with strong canines oppressing his lower lip, a nose neatly broken and sloppily joined. This was Jim Sunn and he was kind to Eddie. "Because he's no trouble to me, Mr. Teitelbaum, he's a good boy. If he opens his eyes wide, I know he wants to go to the bathroom. He ain't crazy, Mr. Teitelbaum, he just got nothing to say right now, is all. I seen a lot of cases, don't you worry."

Mr. Teitelbaum didn't have too much to say himself, and this made him feel united with Eddie. He came every Sunday and sat with him in silence on a bench in the garden behind A Home; in bad weather they met in the parlor, a jolly rectangle scattered with small hooked rugs. They sat for one hour opposite one another in comfortable chairs, peaceful people, then Eddie opened his eyes wide and Jim Sunn said, "O.K. Let's go, buddy. Shut-eye don't hurt the kings of the jungle. Bears hibernate." Mr. Teitelbaum stood on his tiptoes and enfolded Eddie in his arms. "Sonny, don't worry so much," he said, then went home.

This situation prevailed for two years. One cold winter day Mr. Teitelbaum had the flu and couldn't visit. "Where the hell's my father?" Eddie growled.

That was the opener. After that Eddie said other things. Before the week had ended, Eddie said, "I'm sick of peppers, Jim. They give me gas."

A week later he said, "What's the news? Long Island sink yet?"

Dr. Tully had never anticipated Eddie's return. ("Once they go up this road, they're gone," he had confided to the newspapermen.) He invited a consultant from a competing but friendly establishment. He was at last able to give Eddie a Rorschach, which restored his confidence in his original pessimism.

"Let him have more responsibility," the consultant

suggested, which they did at once, allowing him because of his background to visit the A Home For Boys'
Zoo. He was permitted to fondle a rabbit and tease two
box turtles. There was a fawn, caged and sick. Also a
swinging monkey, but Eddie didn't bat an eyelash. That
night he vomited. "What's with the peppers, Jimmy?
Can't that dope cook? Only with peppers?"

Dr. Tully explained that Eddie was now a helper. As
soon as there was a vacancy, he would be given sole responsibility for one animal. "Thank God," Mr. Teitelbaum said. "A dumb animal is a good friend."

At last a boy was cured, sent home to his mother; a
vacancy existed. Dr. Tully considered this a fortunate
vacancy, for the cured boy had been in charge of the
most popular snake in the zoo. The popularity of the
snake had made the boy very popular. The popularity
of the boy had increased his self-confidence; he had become vice-president of the Boys' Assembly; he had ac-
quired friends and sycophants, he had become happy,
cured, and had been returned to society.

On the very first day Eddie proved his mettle. He
cleaned the cage with his right hand, holding the snake
way out with his left. He had many admirers immediately.

"When you go home, could I have the job?" asked a
very pleasant small boy who was only mildly retarded,
but some father was willing to lay out a fortune because
he was ashamed. "I'm not going anywhere, sonny," said
Eddie. "I like it here."

On certain afternoons, shortly after milk and cookies,
Eddie had to bring a little white mouse to his snake. He
slipped the mouse into the cage, and that is why this

snake was so popular: the snake did not eat the mouse immediately. At four o'clock the boys began to gather. They watched the mouse cowering in the corner. They watched the lazy snake wait for his hungry feelings to tickle him all along his curly interior. Every now and then he hiked his spine and raised his head, and the boys breathed hard. Sometime between four-thirty and six o'clock he would begin to slither aimlessly around the cage. The boys laid small bets on the time, winning and losing chunks of chocolate cake or a handful of raisins. Suddenly, but without fuss (and one had to be really watching), the snake stretched his long body, opened his big mouth, and gulped the little live mouse, who always went down squeaking.

Eddie could not disapprove, because this was truly the nature of the snake. But he pulled his cap down over his eyes and turned away.

Jimmy Sunn told him at supper one night, "Guess what I heard. I heard you're acquiring back your identity. Not bad."

"My identity?" asked Eddie.

A week later Eddie handed in a letter of resignation. He sent a copy to his father. The letter said: "Thank you, Dr. Tully. I know who I am. I am no mouse killer. I am Eddie Teitelbaum, the Father of the Stink Bomb, and I am known for my Dedication to Cause and my Fearlessness in the Face of Effect. Do not bother me any more. I have nothing to say. Sincerely."

Dr. Tully wrote a report in which he pointed with pride to his consistent pessimism in the case of Eddie Teitelbaum. This was considered remarkable, in the face of so much hope, and it was remembered by his peers.

While Eddie was making the decision to go out of his mind as soon as possible, other decisions were being made elsewhere. Mr. Teitelbaum, for instance, decided to die of grief and old age—which frequently overlap—and that was the final decision for all Teitelbaums. Shmul sat down to think and was disowned by his father.

Arnold ran away to East Twenty-ninth Street, where he built up a lovely bordello of naked oils at considerable effort and expense.

But Carl, the son of Clop, had tasted with Eddie's tongue. He went to school and stayed for years in order to become an atomic physicist for the Navy. Nowadays on the 8:07 Carl sails out into the hophead currents of our time, fights the undertow with little beep-beep signals. He has retained his cheerful disposition and for this service to the world has just received a wife who was washed out of the Rockettes for being too beautiful.

The War Attenuator has been bottled weak under pressure. It is sometimes called Teitelbaum's Mixture, and its ingredients have been translated into Spanish on the label. It is one of the greatest bug killers of all time. Unfortunately it is sometimes hard on philodendrons and old family rubber plants.

Mrs. Goredinsky still prefers to have her kitchen protected by the Segregator. An old-fashioned lady, she drops in bulk to her knees to scrub the floor. She cannot help seeing the cockroach caught and broiled in his own juice by the busy A.C. She flicks the cockroach off the wall. She smiles and praises Eddie.

The Floating Truth

The day I knocked, all the slats were flat. "Where are you, Lionel?" I shouted. "In the do-funny?"

"For goodness' sake, be quiet," he said, unlatching the back door. "I'm the other side of the coin."

I nicked him with my forefinger. "You don't ring right, Charley. You're counterfeit."

"Come on in and settle," he said. "Keep your hat on. The coat rack's out of order."

I had visited before. The seats were washable plaid plastic—easy to care for—and underfoot was the usual door-to-door fuzz. In graceful disarray philodendrons rose and fell from the back window ledge.

"How in the world can you see to drive, Marlon?"

"Well, baby, I don't drive it much," he said. "It isn't safe."

He offered me an apple from the glove compartment.

"Nature's toothbrush," I said dreamily. "How've you been, Eddie?"

He sighed. "Things never looked better."

He hopped out the front door and crawled in the rear. He was not a seat climber. "Truthfully, I would have phoned you no later than tonight," he said. He snapped the blinds horizontal, and from the east the morning glared at our pale faces. He took a paper and pencil out of a small mahogany file cabinet built along the rear of the front seat. "Let's get down to brass tacks," he said. "What do you want to do?"

"What does anyone want to do?"

"Let me ask the questions," he said. "What do *you* want to do?"

"Oh . . . something worth-while," I said. "Well, make a contribution . . . you know what I mean . . . help out somehow . . . do good."

"Please!" he said bitterly. "Don't waste my time. Every sonofabitch wants to do good."

"Why, that's nice," I said. "What a wonderful social trend. In these terrible times it's marvelous news."

"It's marvelous news . . ." he squeaked in a high girl-voice. "Don't be an idiot. All of time is terrible. You should have lived in a little farming village during the Hundred Years' War. Anyway, do you realize you're paying me by the hour? Let's get started. What can you *do?*"

I was surprised to hear that I was paying him by the hour. Still, for all I know, despite their appearance, these times may not be terrible at all.

"I can type. I went to business school for three months and I can type."

"Don't worry," he said. "I've gotten jobs for virgins. I could place a pediatrician in the Geriatric Clinic."

"If you're so great, Bubbles, how come you don't even have a home?"

"I've only just found myself," he said, turning inward. On the outside he was a mirror image of a face with a dead center. His eyes were blue. The pupils were dark and immovable. He never saw anything out of the corner of his eye but swiveled his whole head to stare at it.

His hair was blond, darkening in a terrible rush before the gray could become general. All his sex characteristics were secondary, which did not prevent him from asking me after our first day's work, "Give me a bunny hug, baby?" I didn't mind at all and did, goosing him gently. It seemed to me he'd like that a lot. I am not considered wild, but I am kind.

I scraped a ham sandwich out of my dungarees and offered him half. "*Gasoline* is what I need," he said peevishly. "I was going to call for a man who invited me to La Vie for a business deal."

Just then the phone rang. He lunged over the front seat for it. "What good luck, Edsel," he chortled. "You got me just as I was pulling up to a meter. Hold it a moment while I disengage." He made grunting noises as though great effort were involved because of tonnage, then resumed his conversation. "Yes? About tonight? I'm not sure I can make it . . . I've got to be out all day . . ."

I waved a one-dollar bill across the windshield mirror. "Ah . . . make it quarter to ten, so I have time to eat. . . . No, that's not necessary . . . No . . . Well, if you insist, at least allow me to call for you. I'll stop by at eight-thirty. . . . Great . . . It'll be marvelous to talk with you again. *A rivederci.*"

"Here," I said, "is a dollar. Petrol."

"I appreciate it," he said.

The Edsel he met at eight-thirty, honking his horn before a canopied doorman, was Jonathan Stubblefield, but don't try to reach him because he's unlisted. His eyes were pale as the moon. They drove here and yon, hip-flasked, unwatered and unsodaed, uniced and defrosted, looped in one another's consonants. Lack of communication made them appear to be lovers.

"Do you have a friend?" asked Jonathan Stubblefield. "Yes, a girl," said my pal, his nose always to the grindstone. Jonathan Stubblefield misunderstood. "Hotcha!" he replied. "I have a friend myself, but the goddamn family— What do you think of the family?" he asked, trying to make sense of his entire life.

"The Family of Man? Oh, I believe in it. But look here, Edsel . . . this girl I'm talking about is not a sexual partner. She's a business associate. Lively, alert, young, charming, clever, enthusiastic. How can you use her?"

"Oh boy," said Jonathan Stubblefield, stupefied. "Upside down, cross-country, her choice. Any way she says."

"You still misunderstand me. It's her business affairs I'm in charge of."

"Oh," said Jonathan Stubblefield. "Oh," he said, "in that case send me a résumé," and passed out.

"But you didn't tell him anything about me," I complained the following afternoon.

"Why should I? He didn't tell me anything about himself. Do you think his real name is Stubblefield? What's the matter with you? Don't put yourself on a platter. What are you—a roast duck, everything removable with a lousy piece of flatware? Be secret. Turn over on your side. Let them guess if you're stuffed. That's how I got where I am."

The organization of his ideas was all wrong; I was drawn to the memory of myself—a mere stripling of a girl—the day I learned that the shortest distance between two points is a great circle.

"Anyway, you ought to think in shorter sentences," he suggested, although I hadn't said a word. Old Richard-the-Liver-Headed, he saw right through to the heart of the matter, my syntax.

"Well, now, just go somewhere for a couple of days. Home, maybe. How about home? Go to the movies. I don't give a damn where you go. I'll have the résumé ready. I've pinpointed Edsel. He's avid to have an employee."

"I'll do what you say." I had to get started somehow. I had been out of school six weeks and was beginning to feel nearly unemployable.

I ducked out of the car. A cop came to the door and squinted authoritatively. "Listen, Squatface, I told you Tuesday, get this hearse to a mummery." He was one of those college cops, in it for the pension. Security is an essential. How else face the future?

"Ran out of gas," my chum whispered as soft as soup.

"Here's a dollar," I replied. "More petrol."

It rained for three days. On the fourth morning, I received a telegram. PHONE OUT OF ORDER. MEET ME USUAL PLACE. SEE EDSEL. LIKE FLYNN, YOU'RE IN.

At noon I found them admiring new white tires. (These are the good times.) I was all dressed up and they were all dressed up. Jonathan Stubblefield observed me. His eyes *were* pale as the moon. He winked and a tear rolled down his smooth cheek. "I have an occluded lachrymal duct," he explained.

"Let's go to the Vilamar Cafeteria where we can talk." He added with pride, "It's on me."

We proceeded at once, single file, Stubblefield leading. In the cafeteria we seated ourselves deferentially around a rotating altar of condiments and began in communal reverence.

"You seem so young," said Jonathan Stubblefield. "I can't really believe that time has passed. Take a good look at me. A man of thirty-one. Inside my head, a photostatic account of Pearl Harbor. I can still see it so clear . . . the snow just stippling the rocks——"

"Snow?"

"Snow. The absolute quiet and then that wild hum and then the noise. And then the whole world plunged into disaster."

"Oh my!"

"You were too young. But I remember—Geneva, Yalta, the San Francisco conference, much-scoffed-at Acheson; those days were the hope of the world. I remember it like yesterday."

"You do?"

"What sort of memories can you young people of today have? You have a reputation for clothes and dope. You have no sense of history; you have no tragic sense. What is Alsace-Lorraine? Can you tell me, my dear? What problem does it face, even today? You don't know. Not innocent, but ignorant."

"You're right," I said.

"Of course," he said. "You can't deny it. The truth finds its own level and floats."

"Coffee?" asked Roderick the middleman.

"Not me," said Edsel. "Baked apple for me. And salmon salad. Jello maybe. I'm on a diet." He patted his tummy. "Now tell me about yourself. I want to know you better."

I tossed my pony tail, agleam with natural oils, and said: "What can I say?"

"You can tell me about yourself. Who you are, where you come from, what your interests are, your hobbies. Who's your favorite boy friend, for instance?"

I told him who I was, where I came from, what my interests and my hobbies were. "But I'm still waiting for Mr. Right to come out of the West."

"You and I have a lot in common," he said sadly. "I'm still waiting for Mr. Right too. I'm paraphrasing, of course. I mean Miss Right.

"You know, you dress beautifully. You look like a rose. Yes, a rose is what is indicated." He touched gently that part of the décolletage furthest from my chin.

He looked at his watch, which had a barometer tucked in somewhere along its circumference. "Pressure rising; I've got to run. Tell our friend 'excuse me' for me. Tell him you're hired, pending résumé. I've got to have that résumé. I don't do business without documentation."

He stood up and transported his gaze slowly from the lady's rest room to the steam counter, the short order table, the grand coffee urns, and finally to the great doors which rested where their rubber stoppers had established them.

"I am lord of all I survey," he murmured. He smiled beneficently on my shining face, then turned on his heels, like the sound of the old order changing, and disappeared into the Götterdämmerung of the revolving doors.

"Oh, Everett, what an interesting man!" I said. We split the salmon salad, but jello reminds me of junket.

"Well, what do you think of him? Not bad. He's the wave of the future. A man who can use leisure. Here's the résumé." He was very businesslike and continued, as he buttered a hard seeded roll, to give me orders for my own good. "Type it. Do a nice job . . . only it has to look home-typed; the only one of its kind. Maybe you ought to make a mistake. If he thinks you've plastered the city with them, you're finished . . . Look it over. It's a day's work, and I'm kind of proud of it."

I riffled and read. "Say, it's three pages, legal size. Do you know it's three pages?"

"Aha!" he said in pride.

"Oh, please, it's ridiculous. What'll I do if he calls any of these people?"

"No, no, no. He *wants* to hire you. He's crazy about you; he wants to be your friend. When he sees all these words, he'll be happy and feel free. He may not even read them."

I looked it over again. These are only a few of the jobs with which he had papered my past. The first, in advertising:

THE GREEN HOUSE: In eight exciting months I brought THE GREEN HOUSE'S name before the public in seven ways—all inexpensive: Two-color posters were distributed. No copy used. A green house on an eggshell-white background. Two-color matchbooks—no copy. Two-color personal cards for all personnel. THE GREEN HOUSE itself was finally painted green. Here and there throughout the city where people least expected it (park benches, lamp posts, etc.), the question asked in green paint: What Is Green? In infinitesimal

green print below and to the right the reply: THE
GREEN HOUSE is green.

"What in hell is THE GREEN HOUSE?"

"I don't know," he giggled.

Here's another; this, under the heading of Public Relations:

The Philadelphia: An association of professionals
working in the Law and allied fields hired me to bring
Law and its possibilities to women everywhere. I trav-
eled throughout the country for five months by bus,
station wagon, train, and also by air under the name
of Gladys Hand. Within nine months there were 11 per
cent more users of legal services. The average fee had
jumped $7.20 over the previous year. Crowded court
calendars required statute revisions in seven states. *The
Philadelphia* ascribed these improvements to my work
in their behalf.

And more:

THE KITCHEN INSTITUTE: Through the medium
of The Kitchen Institute Press's "The Kettle Calls," we
inaugurated a high-pressure plan to return women to
the kitchen. "The kitchen you are leaving may be your
home," was one of many slogans used. By radio and
television, as well as by ads taken in Men's publications
and on Men's pages in newspapers (sports, finance,
etc.), Men were told to ask their wives as they came in
the door each night: "What's cooking?" In this way the
prestige of women in kitchens everywhere was en-
hanced and the need and desire for kitchens accel-
erated.

At the very end, as though it were of no importance
whatsoever, he had typed "More Facts" and then listed:

Single, twenty-three, Grad. Green Valley College for Women. Additional Courses, Sorbonne, in Short Story Writing and Public Speaking. Social Chairman of G O in High School.

"Oh, for God's sake," I said. "That last is pretty silly."

"It may be silly to you, but if he reads it at all he'll certainly read the last line and he'll like that. 'A girl who was lightheaded enough to be social chairman in high school may still be spinning,' is the way I see it."

"But listen," I told him two days later. "I'm not twenty-three."

"You will be, you will be," he assured me.

That afternoon I was helping him water the philodendrons. I was a little excited about being on the threshold of my future, and some water dripped down the back seat and filled the crevices of the upholstery.

"My God, you infuriate me sometimes," he said, tearing the watering can from my hand. "Can't you watch what you're doing?" Poor Dick, he was a covey of twittering angers. "You're so damn stupid!" he screamed. He poured the dregs into an open ash tray and sprinkled the windows. "Get something, get something," he cried. I ran down to the store and bought an old Sunday *Times* to help clean up the mess. I realized that, against great odds, he was only trying to make a home. When I returned he was on the phone: "Can't have you down here. Place is incredible! Let me pick you up. I want to close the deal. It's been pending too long . . . I said 10 per cent . . . 10 per cent is what I want. That's not excessive."

"What deal?" I asked.

"Big deal," he replied sotto voce. "O.K."

The phone rang again. "Edsel!" he beamed. "Long time no see. Long time no hear also . . . Of course," he said. "Ha-ha. 'Can she do shorthand?' Baby, he wants to know if you can do shorthand! Ha-ha, Edsel, she's a speed demon!"

"I can't," I whispered.

He twisted his trunk to reach me and then kicked me on the shin.

He hung up. "O.K.," he said. "Go on over. He's all yours. Good luck. You'll get my bill in the morning mail."

Well, that is how I got my first job. I entered the business world, my senses alert. I quietly watched and voraciously listened. Every 9 A.M. in the five-day week I opened the heavy oak door on which a sign in Old Regal said STUBBLEFIELD. I kept my pencils sharpened. I read the morning papers in the morning and the evening papers in the afternoon, in case some question about current events should arise.

It was true, he had been avid to have an employee and seemed happy. Often his mother called to ask him to please come to lunch or cocktails. Occasionally his father called but left no name. At decent intervals I was instructed to say he was out of town on business. He entrusted me with the key, and when he was away for two or three days, I was in full charge.

I had planned to remain with the job for at least a year, to learn office procedure and persistence.

But one Monday at about 10 A.M. the door opened and a camel-hair blonde, all textured in cashmere, appeared. "I've just been hired by Mr. Stubblefield," she said, "via Western Union." She flapped a manila half

sheet under my nose. "I met him in Bronxville last grad-
uation day." She looked around. There were mauve
walls and army colored file cabinets. "I just love a two-
girl office," she said, expecting to be my friend. "What's
he like? Does he give severance pay?"

She was followed by a desk and a Long Island boy
from the Bell Telephone Company. I didn't say anything to anyone but filed my *Time* and unfolded my
New York *Herald Tribune*. I resharpened my pencil and
proceeded to underline whatever required underlining.

"A lot of paper work?" asked Serena, a cool revision
of my former self. I had nothing to say.

Jonathan Stubblefield poked his snout out of the inner
office. "Get to know each other, girls. You're exactly the
same age."

That information unsettled me.

"You don't know how old I am," I said. "Anyway,
what do you need her for? I'm doing a job. I'm doing as
good a job as you require. This is a deliberate slap in
my face. It is."

"We're in the middle of an expanding economy, for
goodness' sake!" said Jonathan Stubblefield. "Don't be
sentimental. Besides, I thought we could do with some
college people."

"But there isn't enough work to go around," I said
bravely. "There's nothing to do."

"It's my company, isn't it?" he said belligerently. "If
I want to, I can hire forty people to do nothing.
NOTHING."

I looked at Jonathan Stubblefield, a man in tears—but
only because of his lachrymal ducts—a man nevertheless with truth on his side.

"There's room for everybody," he said. But he would not reconsider. He probably never really liked me in the first place.

As I had never used the phone for private conversations, I had to wait until five to call my vocational counselor from a phone booth.

"Come on down, baby," he said, giving me his latitude and longitude. "I don't know what you want to talk about. You owe me fifteen dollars already."

Because of cross-town traffic, it was nearly dark by the time I reached him. I had purchased a rare roast beef sandwich with coleslaw and gift-wrapped it with two green rubber bands. But he laughed in my face. "I only eat out these days; I hate puttering around with drinks and dishes." We gave the sandwich to a passing child who immediately ripped off the aluminum foil and dumped the food into the gutter. She folded the foil neatly and slipped it into her pocket.

Surly Sam turned on the car heater and dimmed the lights. "Oh my," I said, "it's lovely here now. What are those—crocuses?"

"Yes," he said, "crocuses. I take some pride in raising them in the fall."

"Lovely!" I repeated.

"Well," he said, "what's on your mind? How's the job?"

"What job? You call that a job?"

"You're a character!" he said, laying it all at my door. "What'd you expect to do—give polio shots?"

"What's so wrong with that? That's not the most terrible thing in the world."

He entangled all my hopes in one popeyed look. "And

where would you go from there? Let me tell you something. I sent you to Edsel . . . I worked three days on that résumé for him, because I believe that Edsel is going places and anyone on board will be going with him. Believe me, what you're now doing constitutes some of the finest experience available to a young person who wants to set sail for tomorrow.

"Ah yes," he continued philosophically, swiveling slightly to see how absorbent I looked, "ah yes—you could do more. Now if you were really sincere, you could take your shoes off and stand on a street corner with a sign saying: 'He died for me.'" He paused. I didn't comment, because I was waiting for that particular hint that would tell me where I was going, in case it was there. "Or else," he suggested, brightening, "leave the habitations of men—like me."

My heart sank in terror.

He felt he had gone far enough, and we leaned back in the rosy décor, smoking across one artless silence after another. Finally he grimaced out of his usual face, raised an eyebrow, and swiveled. "Ah, what's the use, baby?"

"How true," I said. I owed him something, and in due time I paid him something. Beyond that it was the Sabbath. "It's morning, Morton," I said. "Good night!"

He walked me to the rump of the car.

"I'm not mad," I said. We shook hands and I went my way.

I was directed to the future, but it is hard for me to part with experience. Before I reached the subway entrance, I turned for a last look. He stood in front of the car, glancing up and down the street. There wasn't a soul in his sight. Not even me.

Then he peed. He did not pee like a boy who expects to span a continent, but like a man—in a puddle.

"Good night!" I called, hoping to startle him. He never heard me but stared at the dusty trash he had driven out of the gutters through oblique tunnels that led to the sea. He tightened his belt and hunched his shoulders against the weather. Having left the habitations of men, you can understand he had a special problem. When he was conveniently located he stopped in the city park. At other times he had to use dark one-way streets to help maintain the water levels of this airsick earth.

I gathered fifteen cents from several pockets and started down the subway steps when I heard him shout. In all modesty, I think he was calling me. . . . "Hey, beautiful!" he asseverated. "You're pretty damn diurnal yourself."